Win at Bridge in Thirty Days

by the same author (with Terence Reese)

BRIDGE: THE MODERN GAME

HOW THE EXPERTS DO IT

THE HIDDEN SIDE OF BRIDGE

MIRACLES OF CARD PLAY
(Gollancz)

UNHOLY TRICKS – MORE MIRACULOUS CARD PLAY
(Gollancz)

DOUBLED AND VENERABLE
(Gollancz)

BRIDGE – TRICKS OF THE TRADE
(Gollancz)

Win at Bridge in Thirty Days

David Bird

faber and faber

LONDON · BOSTON

First published in 1990 by
Faber and Faber Limited
3 Queen Square London WCIN 3AU
Reprinted 1990

Typeset by Wilmaset Birkenhead Wirral
Printed in England by Clays Ltd, St Ives plc

A CIP record for this book is
available from the British Library.

ISBN 0-571-14241-9

Contents

Foreword

'Can I really become a good player in thirty days?'

It is certainly possible to take a large step in the right direction. Like anyone who hopes to become a star at golf or snooker, or almost any game, you must start by learning a sound basic technique.

Each of the 'thirty days' consists of two pages on bidding and two pages on play. Study them carefully and at the end you will be a worthy partner for anyone – well on your way towards success at the game.

Day One
(a) The 1NT Opening

When you hold a balanced distribution such as 4–3–3–3 or 4–4–3–2, you will normally bid notrumps, either on the first round or on your first rebid. To measure your hand, use the **point-count** system (ace=4, king=3, queen=2, jack=1). Standards may vary, but the most popular style is that 1NT shows 12–14 points when non-vulnerable, 15–17 when vulnerable. This scheme is known as the **variable notrump**.

The weak notrump

First let's look at the weak notrump (12–14 points). Imagine you are non-vulnerable and you hold one of these hands. Which would represent a sound 1NT opening?

(a)	♠A 1083	(b)	♠K 6	(c)	♠K Q 5
	♡K J 4		♡Q 104		♡A 93
	♢K Q 93		♢Q J 8		♢A 104
	♣9 4		♣A 10763		♣Q 975

On (a) you are happy to open 1NT. The small doubleton in clubs is regrettable, but not enough to dissuade you from the natural opening. Hand (b) is again very suitable for a non-vulnerable 1NT opening. Hands with a 5–3–3–2 distribution, especially when the long suit is a minor, may also be treated as balanced. Hand (c), with 15 points, is too strong for a weak notrump opening. You should open 1♣ and rebid 1NT if partner responds with one of a suit. This sequence, 1 apple – 1 plum – 1NT, suggests the stronger type, 15–17.

The strong notrump

There are hardy types who play the 12–14 notrump throughout, but it is more sensible to demand 15–17 points for a vulnerable notrump.

(a)	♠K 5	(b)	♠A Q J 5	(c)	♠K 62
	♡K Q 4		♡J 3		♡Q 104
	♢A 10832		♢964		♢K 105
	♣K 105		♣A K J 4		♣A J 54

Hand (a) is ideal in every way for a vulnerable opening of 1NT – 15 points, balanced distribution, and a stopper in every suit. The second hand has the values concentrated in two suits and both the red suits are unguarded; you should open 1♣ and rebid 1♠. Hand (c) has insufficient points for a vulnerable 1NT. Open 1♣ and rebid 1NT if partner responds at the one level. This is a relatively weak sequence (12–14) because with a stronger hand, vulnerable, you would have opened 1NT.

A small drawback of the strong notrump is that you are sometimes forced to open on a three-card suit when your point count is 12–14. Imagine you are vulnerable and hold either of these hands:

(a) ♠A43   (b) ♠K954
    ♡KQ62   ♡Q1054
    ◇J84   ◇Q3
    ♣K102   ♣AQ6

If you open 1♡ on (a) you will have no convenient rebid if partner responds 2♣ or 2◇. To rebid 2NT would show more than 13 points, as we shall see later. It is therefore best to open 1♣. If partner responds 1◇ or 1♠ you can rebid 1NT (12–14). If partner responds 1♡ you can raise him to 2♡.

On (b) you might, just, open 1♠, intending to rebid 2♡ over a 2◇ response. It is not at all attractive, however, to open 1♠ on such a threadbare four-card suit. Again the best opening is 1♣.

Such openings on a three-card minor are known, informally, as **prepared** bids. When you are non-vulnerable and are playing a weak notrump, they are needed less frequently. Suppose you have to open a hand like this, though:

♠AK3 ♡J862 ◇AK4 ♣J93

The best choice is 1◇ rather than 1♡, when the major suit is so poor.

(b) Building Tricks

Planning the play in a notrump contract is often fairly simple. You count how many top tricks you have, then try to work out the best way to establish the extra tricks you need. Look at this typical deal:

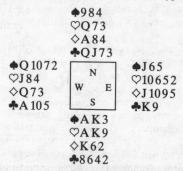

```
              ♠984
              ♡Q73
              ◇A84
              ♣QJ73
♠Q1072    ┌─────────┐   ♠J65
♡J84      │    N    │   ♡10652
◇Q73      │  W   E  │   ◇J1095
♣A105     │    S    │   ♣K9
          └─────────┘
              ♠AK3
              ♡AK9
              ◇K62
              ♣8642
```

West leads ♠2 against 3NT. You can count seven top tricks – two spades, three hearts and two diamonds. You therefore need to establish two more to bring your total to nine. The club suit should produce two tricks, but first you will have to knock out the ace and king of the suit. Win the spade lead and play a club to the queen. East wins with the king and returns a spade. You win this trick and play another club towards dummy's jack. Whether West takes his ♣A on this trick or the next you will score two club tricks. The defenders, meanwhile, will make just two spades and two clubs.

Most notrump contracts present this kind of problem. You count how many tricks you have on top, then see how you can establish the extra tricks you need. Here are some more suit holdings where you can build extra tricks:

(a) ♣AK73   (b) ◇A864   (c) ♡KQ72

    ♣965   ◇7532   ♡853

On (a) you can build one extra trick if the defenders' clubs are divided 3–3. You start by ducking one round of the suit. When you regain the lead you cash the ace and king. If both defenders follow all the way the thirteenth club will be good.

On (b) you must duck two rounds of the suit. Provided the defenders' diamonds are divided 3–2 you will establish an extra trick eventually.

The number of tricks you can make on (c) depends on how the suit breaks and on which defender holds ♡A. You lead twice towards

dummy, hoping that West holds the ace. If West has a holding such as
♡A 10 x you will score three tricks in the suit. If East holds ♡A J x x you
will score only one.

Here is another 3NT contract. How would you build the extra tricks
you need?

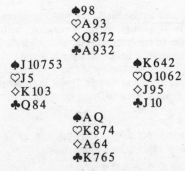

♠98
♡A 9 3
◇Q 8 7 2
♣A 9 3 2

♠J 10 7 5 3   ♠K 6 4 2
♡J 5   ♡Q 10 6 2
◇K 10 3   ◇J 9 5
♣Q 8 4   ♣J 10

♠A Q
♡K 8 7 4
◇A 6 4
♣K 7 6 5

West leads ♠5 against your 3NT and you win East's king with the ace.
You can count seven top tricks – two spades, two hearts, one diamond
and two clubs. You need two more. A possible play would be to duck a
round of clubs. Because the suit breaks 3–2 this would establish an extra
trick for you. One extra trick is not enough, though; when the defenders
took their club trick they would clear the spade suit. Eight tricks would
be your limit.

You must look for a suit that may yield two additional tricks. This is
possible only in diamonds and to succeed you will need to find a 3–3
break and ◇K onside. So, cash ◇A and play a diamond towards
dummy. West will doubtless take his ◇K and clear the spades, but nine
tricks are yours.

Day Two
(a) Responding to 1NT

When your partner has opened 1NT you know to within a point or two how strong he is. It is therefore fairly easy for you to tell if you have the values for game between you. Around 25 points are enough for a notrump game, slightly fewer if there is a long suit that will provide tricks. We shall look separately at the cases where you decide (a) no game is possible, (b) game may be possible if partner has a maximum, and (c) you definitely want to be in game.

Signing off

Suppose your partner has opened a non-vulnerable (12–14) 1NT. What would you respond on each of these hands?

(a) ♠106
    ♡J65
    ◇K542
    ♣8432

(b) ♠AK5
    ♡84
    ◇Q973
    ♣J852

(c) ♠J9654
    ♡1052
    ◇Q532
    ♣4

(d) ♠4
    ♡AQ1054
    ◇1096
    ♣K952

No problem on (a); you simply pass 1NT. The same is true of hand (b). You and your partner have 22–24 points (out of 40) between you; at best, nine tricks will be a struggle.

On hand (c) you know that game is not possible, but this hand is likely to play better in spades than in notrumps. Bid 2♠, which your partner will pass. A further reason for bidding 2♠ is that you make it more difficult for opponents to compete. Hand (d) might, on a good day, produce ten tricks in hearts, but a simple 2♡ is best nevertheless.

Inviting a game

When the combined total might reach the magic 25, you can invite a game. Suppose that your partner, vulnerable, has opened a 15–17 1NT and you hold either of these hands:

(a) ♠A103
    ♡103
    ◇Q976
    ♣K982

(b) ♠K5
    ♡874
    ◇KQ963
    ♣J104

In each case you can raise to 2NT, inviting partner to bid 3NT unless he holds a minimum.

Advancing to game

When you judge the partnership has enough to attempt a game you can either bid a game directly or make a suit response at the three level. Such bids are forcing and invite partner to co-operate in choosing the best game. How would you respond to a 12–14 1NT on these hands?

(a) ♠A Q 3
    ♡K J 4
    ◇Q 8 5
    ♣Q 10 6 4

(b) ♠4
    ♡A 10 2
    ◇A K 10 7 6 5
    ♣J 9 5

(c) ♠A K J 9 8 2
    ♡6
    ◇Q 5 4
    ♣10 9 5

(d) ♠A 4
    ♡A Q 9 8 2
    ◇K 10 5 3
    ♣8 3

On (a) you and your partner can lay claim to at least 26 points between you. Give him the good news by jumping to 3NT. Again, on (b) you should raise to 3NT. Don't think of looking for a diamond game; nine tricks are usually easier to make than eleven. On hand (c) your splendid spade suit will bring in several tricks; bid 4♠.

The fourth hand (d) is not so straightforward. You want to be in game, but which game? If partner has three or more hearts, game in that suit will probably be easier to make than 3NT. Bid 3♡. This call is forcing to game and asks your partner to choose between 3NT and 4♡. Usually he will bid 3NT when he has a doubleton heart, 4♡ otherwise.

Here is a typical auction involving a 3-level response:

West	East	West	East
♠A 4	♠K J 10 7 2	1NT	3♠[1]
♡Q J 7 4	♡K 10 8 5 3	3NT[2]	4♡[3]
◇Q 7 4	◇6	No[4]	
♣K Q 9 3	♣A 4		

[1] I have five spades and enough points for game.
[2] Only two spades here, I'm afraid; better play in notrumps.
[3] I have five hearts, too. Do you like those any better?
[4] I certainly do.

(b)   Planning a Suit Contract

Suppose you are South on the deal below, playing in six spades. West leads ♡K. How would you plan the contract?

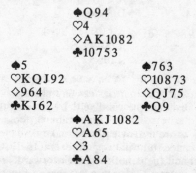

```
                ♠Q94
                ♡4
                ◇AK1082
                ♣10753
 ♠5                          ♠763
 ♡KQJ92                      ♡10873
 ◇964                        ◇QJ75
 ♣KJ62                       ♣Q9
                ♠AKJ1082
                ♡A65
                ◇3
                ♣A84
```

First, count your top tricks. You have six spades, one heart, two diamonds and a club. That makes ten altogether. You can make two more tricks by ruffing two hearts in the dummy. This will bring your total to twelve.

You win ♡A and ruff a heart. Then you return to the South hand with a trump and ruff another heart. There are no trumps left in dummy, so you cross to ♣A to draw the opponents' remaining trumps. Finally you play ◇AK, discarding one of your club losers. All you lose is one club trick at the end.

Another way of planning a suit contract is to look at the losers in the long trump hand (here South). Look back at the South hand. You have no losers in spades, two losers in hearts (♡65), no losers in diamonds, and two losers in clubs (♣84). You have a total of four losers and need to take care of three of them. Here you can ruff two hearts and discard one of the club losers – no problem.

Try planning this six-heart contract. West leads ◇Q.

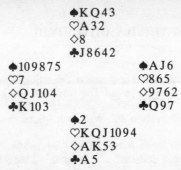

♠KQ43
♡A32
◇8
♣J8642

♠109875   ♠AJ6
♡7   ♡865
◇QJ104   ◇9762
♣K103   ♣Q97

♠2
♡KQJ1094
◇AK53
♣A5

Count your winners first. You have six hearts, two diamonds and a club – a total of only nine. You can bump this to eleven by ruffing two diamonds in the dummy; and a twelfth trick will come by establishing a spade winner. So, win the diamond lead and play a spade to the king. Say that East wins and returns a club. You win with the ace, ruff a diamond with a low trump and return to hand with a trump to the king. Ruff your other diamond loser with the ace of trumps, discard a club on ♠Q, and ruff a spade high to re-enter the South hand. Then draw the outstanding trumps and claim the remaining tricks.

Now try the other method of planning the contract, by concentrating on the losers in the long trump hand. You have four losers (one in spades, two in diamonds and one in clubs) and must dispose of three of them. You plan to do this by ruffing two diamonds and discarding a club.

Here is a final example, six clubs on a low diamond lead:

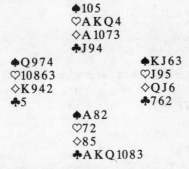

♠105
♡AKQ4
◇A1073
♣J94

♠Q974   ♠KJ63
♡10863   ♡J95
◇K942   ◇QJ6
♣5   ♣762

♠A82
♡72
◇85
♣AKQ1083

There are eleven tricks on top and you can make a twelfth by ruffing a spade in dummy. Win the diamond lead and draw one round of trumps. Then you must aim to cash the three heart winners, discarding your diamond loser. When the weather stays fine you give the defenders a spade trick, preparing for your ruff. You win their return, ruff a spade and return to the South hand to draw trumps.

Day Three
(a) The Stayman Convention

When partner opens 1NT a response of 2♣ is **Stayman**, named after the American player Sam Stayman. The response invites opener to bid a four-card major. Holding no four-card major, the opener rebids 2♢. If he has four hearts he rebids 2♡. With four spades, and not four hearts, he rebids 2♠.

See how this convention works on the deals below. Assume that East-West are vulnerable and that a 1NT opening therefore shows 15–17 points.

West	East	West	East
♠A Q 9 2	♠J 3	1NT[1]	2♣[2]
♡Q J 2	♡A 10 5 4	2♠[3]	3NT[4]
♢A 5 4	♢K 10 8 3		
♣A 10 2	♣K 7 5		

[1] I have a balanced hand of 15–17 points, partner.
[2] Great! Have you a four-card major?
[3] Yes, in spades, but not in hearts.
[4] We'd better play in 3NT, then.

Stayman on game hands

Here are some more sequences that use Stayman on the way to game:

West	East	West	East
♠J 64	♠A 5	1NT	2♣
♡K Q 9 2	♡A J 8 4	2♡	4♡
♢A K 8 3	♢762		
♣A 5	♣Q 9 7 2		

East-West reach 4♡, a sounder contract than 3NT.

West	East	West	East
♠A Q 9 4	♠K J 8 3	1NT	2♣
♡A J 6 5	♡K 7	2♡	3NT
♢Q J 4	♢A 10 5 2	4♠	
♣K 5	♣842		

When East bids 3NT at his second turn West must ask himself, 'Why did partner use Stayman?' There is only one possible reason – because he has four spades. West therefore advances to the spade game over 3NT.

Stayman on game-try hands

Sometimes the responder will be slightly weaker than in the above examples. He may have the values for a game try but want to investigate a major fit on the way.

West	East	West	East
♠AK84	♠QJ72	1NT	2♣
♡K94	♡A83	2♠	3♠
◇K105	◇Q862	No	
♣Q73	♣92		

Here East finds a 4–4 spade fit and invites partner to bid game if he has values to spare. West, with an unappetizing minimum, is content to pass three spades.

If West's rebid had been 2◇ or 2♡, East's second call would be 2NT, still invitational.

How can you make a game try when you hold a 5- or 6-card major? We have already seen that an immediate response such as 3♠ would be game-forcing. To invite game you must bid three of a major *via* Stayman:

West	East	West	East
♠K84	♠AQ7652	1NT	2♣
♡AJ73	♡8	2◇	3♠
◇AJ94	◇1072	4♠	
♣A3	♣J94		

East's 3♠, via Stayman, is non-forcing, but invites partner to advance if his hand is suitable. Here West has three-card support, three aces and a side-suit doubleton. He happily accepts the invitation.

Stayman on part-score hands

You can sometimes use Stayman to find a playable spot at the two-level. This is safe only when no response will embarrass you. Suppose your partner has opened a 12–14 notrump and you hold one of these hands:

(a) ♠A54	(b) ♠Q10852	(c) ♠KJ54
♡Q954	♡AJ74	♡8
◇J10763	◇5	◇A1062
♣4	♣965	♣J853

Stayman will work well on (a). If partner responds 2◇ or 2♡, this will normally be a more productive spot than 1NT. Even if he responds 2♠ this is likely to play as least as well as 1NT.

Stayman is right, too, on (b). If partner says 2◇, denying a 4-card major, you will bid 2♠. This is not invitational. Hand (c) is unsuitable for Stayman; you would have nowhere to run if partner rebid 2♡.

(b) Finessing

There is not much skill involved in making a trick with an ace, but other honours may need skilful handling. Often this involves no more than leading *towards* honour combinations. These are simple positions:

(a) KQ3   (b) KQJ6   (c) Q64

764   852   973

With holding (a) you must lead twice towards the king-queen. If West has the ace you will score two tricks, otherwise only one. The second combination is similar. If West has Axxx you may need to lead three times towards the dummy. Prospects on (c) are not good, but if you lead twice towards dummy's queen you will score a trick whenever West holds both the ace and king.

Two types of finesse

When the opponents hold the king of a suit there are two basic ways you can finesse against it:

(a) AQ   (b) A6   (c) A52

63   QJ   Q83

In position (a) you lead towards the honours, playing dummy's queen when West follows with a low card. Holding (b) is slightly different because you lead a high card from the South hand. If West holds the king you will again score two tricks without loss. It would be silly to lead the queen in (c). West will cover if he holds the king and you will score only one trick. To make two tricks you must lead towards the queen, hoping that East has the king.

In general you should not lead a high card to a finesse unless you are sure you won't mind if the high card is covered. Look at these positions:

(a) AQ75   (b) AQ7652

J643   J43

Suppose that you need four tricks from (a). It is pointless to lead the jack. West will cover if he holds the king and you will never score four tricks in the suit. Play low to the queen instead, continuing with the ace if the finesse succeeds. You will score four tricks when West started with Kx. It is the same with (b). Lead a low card, not the jack, which would cost if West had a singleton king and East 10xx.

Combination finesses

Sometimes you can take two finesses in one suit. These are common holdings:

(a) A J 10   (b) A J 9   (c) A Q 9

754   632   742

On (a) you lead towards the honours, playing the jack unless West inserts an honour. If the first finesse loses you can finesse the 10 next time. Unless East holds both the king and the queen (which happens only 25 per cent of the time), you will score two tricks in the suit.

With (b) you begin with a deep finesse of the 9. If West started with K 10 x or Q 10 x, the 9 will force a high honour from East. A subsequent finesse of dummy's jack will bring you a second trick in the suit. You make a similar start, a deep finesse of the 9, on (c). If West started with J 10 x you gain a trick, as the 9 will force the king.

These are examples of a double finesse:

(a) A Q 10   (b) K J 7

752   843

On (a) you start with a deep finesse of the 10. You score three tricks if West started with both the missing honours. If the 10 loses to the jack you can finesse again for the king. The same principle applies to (b). Finesse the lower honour, the jack, on the first round.

The two-way finesse

Sometimes you can finesse either opponent for a missing queen. Look at these common holdings:

(a) A 10 3   (b) A 8 2

K J 4   K J 10

If you think West has the queen on (a) you can finesse dummy's 10. Should you place East with the missing queen you can finesse the jack instead. As a rule, there will be some indication. One defender may be more likely than the other to hold a particular high card, or just more likely to hold length.

With (b) you can try a well-known gambit. Lead the jack from the South hand, tempting West to cover with the queen. If he plays low in unconcerned fashion, you rise with dummy's king and finesse the 10 on the way back.

Day Four
(a) Opening One of a Suit

We have already seen that with a balanced hand you will either open with a notrump call or rebid in notrumps, depending on your strength. Most other hands (except those which are exceptionally strong) will be opened one of a suit. Usually you will open one of your longest suit:

(a) ♠104　　(b) ♠K5　　(c) ♠K10765
　　♡AQ1082　　♡6　　　　♡Q5
　　◇KJ54　　　◇AQ1084　　◇9
　　♣A2　　　　♣KQ972　　♣AKJ84

On (a) you open 1♡, intending to rebid 2◇ if partner responds in a black suit. On (b) you have two five-card suits. In this case you should normally open the **higher** suit. Here you open 1◇, intending to rebid 2♣. There is one exception to this rule – when you hold clubs and spades, as in (c), it is best to open 1♣, intending to rebid 1♠.

You will gather from the discussion above that whenever you open one of a suit you must consider what your rebid will be. This is particularly true when you do not hold a five-card suit. Look at these hands, assuming you are vulnerable and first to speak.

(a) ♠K4　　(b) ♠J92
　　♡AQ72　　♡AK104
　　◇972　　　◇AJ83
　　♣A1054　　♣104

If you open 1♡ on (a) you will have no convenient rebid if partner responds 2◇ (to rebid 2NT would suggest 15–16 points and you have only 13). You should therefore open 1♣, intending to rebid 1NT over a response of 1♠.

On (b) a 1◇ opening would leave you with no good rebid if partner responded 2♣. It is better to open 1♡; then you can rebid 2◇ over 2♣.

(c) ♠J1083　　(d) ♠KQ93
　　♡5　　　　　♡KJ104
　　◇AQ72　　　◇AJ85
　　♣AK95　　　♣2

On most hands with 4–4–4–1 distribution it works well to open in the suit below the singleton; 1◇ on hand (c), for example. The exception is when the singleton is in clubs, as in (d). On this type a 1♡ opening is the best idea.

The limits of an opening one-bid

Opening bids of one of a suit cover a wide range in terms of high-card points. If you have a good suit or perhaps two good suits, you may open on as few as 10 points. Each of these hands represents a sound opening bid at any score:

(a) ♠AQ10964   (b) ♠6   (c) ♠972
    ♡72   ♡AQ10542   ♡—
    ◇A863   ◇KJ865   ◇AKQJ5
    ♣5   ♣7   ♣109863

Opening bids of 1♠, 1♡, and 1◇, respectively, would be standard practice on these hands. Reverse the minor suits on (c) and it would still be reasonable to open 1◇.

The maximum point-count for a one-level opening in a suit is around 19 or even 20 points. These hands represent the top of the range:

(a) ♠AQ32   (b) ♠KJ   (c) ♠Q5
    ♡AQJ4   ♡J10872   ♡9862
    ◇6   ◇AKQJ4   ◇AKQ
    ♣KQJ5   ♣A   ♣AKQ2

Hand (a) would be opened 1♣, hand (b) 1♡, and hand (c) 1♣.

As you can see, a one-level suit opening covers a wide range. It is only on the next round of the bidding that you can give partner a better idea of your strength. How this is done we will see on Day Eight.

(b) How to Establish a Suit

When you have a long suit in dummy it may be possible to **establish** it –
to set up one or more long cards in the suit. Look at this deal:

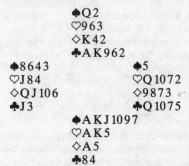

```
              ♠Q2
              ♡963
              ◇K42
              ♣AK962
♠8643                    ♠5
♡J84                     ♡Q1072
◇QJ106                   ◇9873
♣J3                      ♣Q1075
              ♠AKJ1097
              ♡AK5
              ◇A5
              ♣84
```

You reach the excellent contract of seven spades and West leads ◇Q.
There is only one way to avoid losing a heart trick. You must establish a
club trick in dummy and throw your heart loser on it.

Entries to dummy are not plentiful, so you win the diamond lead with
the ace. You then play the ace and king of clubs and ruff a club with a
high trump. West shows out on this trick, so you will need one more
club ruff to establish the suit. You cross to ♠Q and ruff the fourth round
of clubs high. Finally you draw West's trumps and cross to ◇K to take a
heart discard on the good club in dummy.

Do you see why it was necessary to play on clubs before drawing
trumps? Right, because you might need ♠Q as an entry for a second
club ruff. Note also how important it was to ruff the clubs with high
trumps. If at any stage you had ruffed with the 7 West would have
overruffed.

Suppose you are trying to establish a suit such as A x x x x x in the
dummy opposite x x in your own hand. You will have to lose a trick in
the suit sometime. By ducking the *first* round you can preserve the ace
as an entry that will enable you to take a ruff in the suit. You would need
such a play on this deal:

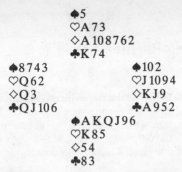

```
            ♠5
            ♡A 7 3
            ◇A 10 8 7 6 2
            ♣K 7 4
♠8 7 4 3                    ♠10 2
♡Q 6 2                      ♡J 10 9 4
◇Q 3                        ◇K J 9
♣Q J 10 6                   ♣A 9 5 2
            ♠A K Q J 9 6
            ♡K 8 5
            ◇5 4
            ♣8 3
```

You play in four spades and West leads ♣Q followed by ♣J, both of which you duck in the dummy. West would do best to switch to hearts now, but he persists with clubs and you ruff the third round. You have lost two tricks in clubs and will certainly lose another in diamonds. To avoid a heart loser you need to establish dummy's diamond suit.

The important play here is to duck the *first* round of diamonds. When East returns ♡J, win with the king, draw trumps, play a diamond to the ace and ruff the third round.

A duck is sometimes necessary even when dummy has two entries in the key suit.

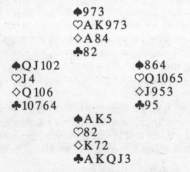

```
            ♠9 7 3
            ♡A K 9 7 3
            ◇A 8 4
            ♣8 2
♠Q J 10 2                   ♠8 6 4
♡J 4                        ♡Q 10 6 5
◇Q 10 6                     ◇J 9 5 3
♣10 7 6 4                   ♣9 5
            ♠A K 5
            ♡8 2
            ◇K 7 2
            ♣A K Q J 3
```

You reach six clubs and West leads ♠Q. There are eleven tricks on top and the twelfth trick will have to come from dummy's heart suit. Suppose you win the spade lead, draw trumps and play ace, king and another heart. If hearts are 3–3 you will score thirteen tricks. If hearts are 4–2, which is more likely, you will go one down.

Instead of playing hearts from the top you should *duck the first round* of the suit. The defenders will probably return a diamond. You win with the king, cross to ♡A and cash ♡K. If hearts prove to be 4–2 you can ruff a heart and return to ◇A to take a discard on the thirteenth heart.

Day Five
(a) Raising Partner's Suit

When partner has launched the ship with an opening bid of one of a suit there are various types of response you can make. In this chapter we consider the situation where you have good trump support for your partner. You will have to judge how valuable your hand is in support and to what level you should raise the bidding.

When to give a single raise

A single raise of partner's opening bid suggests about 6–8 points. Each of these hands would be worth a raise of 1♠ to 2♠:

(a)	♠KJ64	(b)	♠Q105	(c)	♠K1054
	♡Q953		♡6		♡83
	◇K72		◇J6532		◇964
	♣94		♣A854		♣Q962

Hand (a) represents the maximum on which a single raise would be given. Hand (b) has only three-card support in trumps, but contains a singleton (a ruffing value). You bid 2♠, rather than 1NT or two of a minor. You would never raise a minor suit with only three trumps, however.

Partner will not expect such a weak hand as (c) when you give him a single raise. You should make this call, nevertheless, hoping to make life difficult for the opponents, who are sure to have a good fit somewhere. Also, game in spades, though unlikely, may be possible or even lay-down.

Sometimes after a single raise the opener may be uncertain whether to advance to game. In this case he can take advantage of the available space by making a **game try**. He calls a suit where he looks for support. It may be his next longest suit or it may be a weak holding such as x x x.

West	East	West	East
♠94	♠872	1♡	2♡
♡AQJ103	♡K962	3◇	4♡
◇A1054	◇J2		
♣A5	♣K1064		

West's 3◇ is a game try. East has little to spare in terms of high cards, but his diamond shortage suggests that the hands will fit well. West will no doubt be able to ruff at least one diamond loser. If East's diamonds and spades were the other way round he would refuse the try, signing off in 3♡.

When to give a double raise

A double raise, such as 1♠ raised to 3♠, is non-forcing, but encouraging. Partner will advance unless he is minimum. Each of these hands is worth a double raise of a 1♠ opening:

(a) ♠A 1054   (b) ♠KJ 1053   (c) ♠J862
    ♡92   ♡863   ♡86
    ◇KJ62   ◇A853   ◇J5
    ♣K84   ♣2   ♣AK1054

Hand (a) is top weight for a double raise. Add another jack and the scales would topple – you would want to be in game. Hand (b) contains only 8 points, but with five trumps, a side ace and a singleton it is well worth a raise to three. Some players would raise to four on the hand. It would not be a mistake to raise directly to 3♠ on hand (c), but it is slightly more accurate to respond 2♣ on the first round. If partner rebids at the two level you may then bid 3♠. This sequence would be non-forcing, but strongly invitational.

Direct game raise

There are two reasons why you might advance directly to game when partner has opened one of a major. The obvious one is that you think you might make the game. The other is that when you have a relatively weak hand with excellent support for partner, a jump to the four level may silence the opponents, who are sure to have a good fit somewhere themselves. Suppose your partner has opened 1♠ and you have any of these hands:

(a) ♠A 10542 (b) ♠A 109654 (c) ♠AQ72
    ♡Q 1075   ♡6   ♡76
    ◇KJ2   ◇Q74   ◇J103
    ♣5   ♣1053   ♣AKJ4

On (a) you raise to 4♠, expecting to make the contract. On (b) you make the same call. You may or may not make the contract, but the first priority is to gag the opponents. This is called a **pre-emptive** raise. It can hardly be right to make the same responding call on (c) as on (b). To differentiate between the two types, on (c) you respond 2♣, then bid 4♠ on the next round. Such a sequence shows good values and is known as a **delayed game raise**.

(b) Ruffing in the Dummy

When you are playing a trump contract one of the most important decisions is whether to draw trumps immediately. If you are planning to take some ruffs in the dummy you will often have to delay drawing trumps. Have a look at this deal:

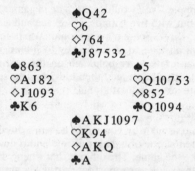

♠Q42
♡6
◇764
♣J87532

♠863   ♠5
♡AJ82   ♡Q10753
◇J1093   ◇852
♣K6   ♣Q1094

♠AKJ1097
♡K94
◇AKQ
♣A

You arrive in six spades and West leads ◇J. You have three heart losers and must plan to ruff two of them in dummy. Obviously it would be foolish to draw the defenders' trumps before you had taken the ruffs. You might be tempted to cross to ♠Q to lead a heart towards the king but even this single round of trumps would prove fatal as the cards lie. West would take ♡K and play a second round of trumps. You would have two hearts to ruff and only one trump left in the dummy.

The winning play is to give up a heart at trick 2. Play ♡9 from the South hand. You can then win the trump return, organize your two heart ruffs and eventually return to the South hand to draw trumps.

Note that the extra tricks on this hand were made by taking ruffs in the **short trump hand**. You made six trump tricks in the South hand and two in the North, a total of eight. You would not gain by ruffing clubs in the long trump hand, since the six trumps in the South hand were winners already.

Avoiding an overruff

When there is a danger that an opponent may overruff you may be able to exhaust the trumps of the critical defender. This deal is a good illustration:

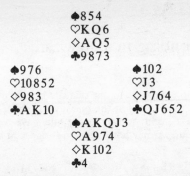

                    ♠854
                    ♡KQ6
                    ◇AQ5
                    ♣9873
    ♠976   ♠102
    ♡10852   ♡J3
    ◇983   ◇J764
    ♣AK10   ♣QJ652
                    ♠AKQJ3
                    ♡A974
                    ◇K102
                    ♣4

You reach an ambitious six spades and West eagerly leads the top
clubs. You ruff the second round and see that you must make plans for
your fourth heart. It may seem that you need a 3–3 break in the suit, but
there is an additional chance that will work if the defender with short
hearts has only two trumps. Play just the ace and king of spades, then
cash the top three hearts. East will be unable to ruff the third round and
you will safely ruff the loser.

Another way to avoid an overruff is by ruffing with a high trump. On
this deal declarer has two spades to ruff and only one high trump in
dummy.

                    ♠54
                    ♡Q53
                    ◇Q10972
                    ♣A94
    ♠Q976   ♠J83
    ♡86   ♡972
    ◇K85   ◇AJ63
    ♣KQJ5   ♣1062
                    ♠AK102
                    ♡AKJ104
                    ◇4
                    ♣873

You reach four hearts and West leads ♣K, won in the dummy. All
follow when you cash the two top spades and you continue with a third
round. It would be foolish to ruff this round with the queen because you
would then be almost certain to suffer an overruff on the fourth round.
Ruff with a low trump, return to hand with a trump and ruff the fourth
round of spades with dummy's last trump, the queen. You can then lead
a diamond, preparing a route back to hand to draw the outstanding
trumps.

Day Six
(a) Responding in a New Suit

The most common response to one of a suit is a bid in a new suit at the minimum level. Such a call at the one level promises no more than 6 points, perhaps a point or two less if you have a long major suit. Suppose that your partner has opened 1◇ and you hold one of these hands:

(a) ♠A754   (b) ♠KJ9852   (c) ♠KQ1083
   ♡Q1054   ♡1082   ♡AJ972
   ◇Q96   ◇54   ◇3
   ♣92   ♣93   ♣A4

On (a) you respond 1♡. Note that you bid the **lower of 4-card-suits** when responding. You can see that this makes sense. Partner can easily introduce a spade suit over your 1♡ response so you will find a fit in either major suit. Had you responded 1♠ it would have been less easy for partner to mention a heart suit.

Hand (b) contains only 4 points but it is safe to respond 1♠. Little damage can come from this and you make it more difficult for the opponents to enter. On hand (c) you respond 1♠, bidding the **higher of 5-card suits**. You intend to bid both suits yourself. By calling spades first, then hearts at some level, you make it easy for partner to express a preference.

When to respond at the two level

To respond at the two level you need as a rule 10 points or so. Suppose that partner has opened 1◇ and you hold either of these hands:

(a) ♠KJ94   (b) ♠AQ73
   ♡K4   ♡1085
   ◇82   ◇6
   ♣AQ1054   ♣Q9862

On (a) you have more than enough to respond at the two level. Bid 2♣ intending to introduce the spades on the next round. Hand (b) has only 8 points, not enough for a two-level response. You keep the bidding alive with a call of 1♠.

A response of 2♡ over 1♠ normally promises a 5-card suit at least. Suppose that partner has opened 1♠ and you hold either of these hands:

(a) ♠53   (b) ♠Q62
   ♡AKJ4   ♡AQ104
   ◇762   ◇982
   ♣QJ93   ♣A103

No problem on (a), you respond 2♣, the lower of your two 4-card suits. On (b) 2♡ will hardly be a disaster, but 2♣ is preferable. If partner raises to 3♣ you can bid 3♢.

When you have a long, strong suit it may be best to bid at the two level even when you are a point or two shy of the normal values:

(a)   ♠5   (b)   ♠J5
     ♡964   ♡KQJ9732
     ◇AQJ1086   ◇1083
     ♣J52   ♣3

Bid 2◇ over 1♠ on (a). If partner rebids 2♡ or 2♠ you can bid rebid 3◇, not a strong call. Similarly you can call 2♡ over 1♠ on (b).

Bid a new suit or raise partner?

When partner opens one of a minor suit you may have to choose between raising him and introducing a new suit. Normally it is right to respond in a major suit. Suppose you have one of these hands, facing a 1♣ opening:

(a)   ♠95   (b)   ♠J972   (c)   ♠1083
     ♡AQ84   ♡J6   ♡62
     ◇1052   ◇983   ◇KJ105
     ♣J962   ♣AQ64   ♣Q942

On (a) prefer a 1♡ response to a raise to 2♣. Do not carry this principle too far, though. On (b) the spades are feathery and it is better to respond 2♣. Make the same response on (c). There is little to be gained by introducing the diamonds and a 2♣ response will make it slightly harder for the opponents to enter the auction.

(b) Taking Discards

We have already seen one situation where declarer may wish to delay drawing trumps: when he needs to take a ruff or two in the short trump hand. Another time is when he needs to take a quick discard. This deal is typical:

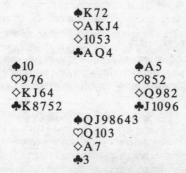

♠K72
♥AKJ4
♦1053
♣AQ4

♠10   ♠A5
♥976   ♥852
♦KJ64   ♦Q982
♣K8752   ♣J1096

♠QJ98643
♥Q103
♦A7
♣3

South reaches a respectable small slam in spades and West strikes a healthy blow for his side by leading a diamond. On any other lead declarer would be able to play on trumps, eventually discarding his diamond loser on dummy's long heart. With the diamond suit exposed by the lead, declarer cannot afford to play on trumps immediately. He wins the diamond lead and, aiming for a quick discard, finesses ♣Q. As it happens, the finesse succeeds. Declarer discards his diamond loser on ♣A and turns happily to the trump suit, soon racking up twelve tricks.

If the club finesse had lost he would have been two down instead of one, but this would be a small premium to pay for the chance of making the slam.

This was another hand where establishing a discard should have taken precedence over drawing trumps:

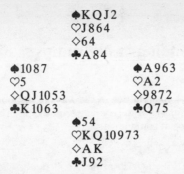

```
                    ♠KQJ2
                    ♡J864
                    ◇64
                    ♣A84
    ♠1087                      ♠A963
    ♡5                         ♡A2
    ◇QJ1053                    ◇9872
    ♣K1063                     ♣Q75
                    ♠54
                    ♡KQ10973
                    ◇AK
                    ♣J92
```

South reached four hearts and won the diamond lead with the ace. He turned straight to the trump suit, leading the king to East's ace. Clubs were the only suit that offered any promise for the defence, so East returned a low club to the 9, 10 and ace. Declarer drew the remaining trump with the queen and, far too late, played a spade towards dummy, aiming to set up a discard. The result was predictable. East won with the ace and the defenders cashed two club tricks to put the game one down.

Declarer should have played on spades at trick 2. If East takes the ace and switches to clubs, declarer can discard one of his club losers on the third round of spades before playing on trumps.

Change North's hand a bit, giving him only KQ62 in spades. It would still be right for declarer to play on spades at trick 2. If *West* held the ace there would be time to establish the vital discard.

25

Day Seven
(a) Responding in Notrumps

We have already looked at two of the ways to respond to one of a suit: you can bid another suit or raise your partner's suit. The third possibility is to call notrumps at some level.

When to respond 1NT

A response of 1NT suggests around 6–9 points. Suppose that your partner has opened 1♡ and you hold one of these hands:

(a) ♠Q82	(b) ♠AJ93	(c) ♠K3
♡54	♡3	♡9
◇AQ64	◇10874	◇A10854
♣10963	♣J1092	♣J9762

Hand (a) is a straightforward response of 1NT. It would not be a mistake to make the same response on (b), but it is preferable to bid a fair major suit if you can do so at the one level. The third hand is not balanced but, as indicated on Day Six, it is not strong enough for a response at the two level. You must therefore respond 1NT.

When to respond 2NT

With a balanced hand of 11–12 points you can respond 2NT, non-forcing. You sometimes have to judge whether it is worth bidding a suit on the way. Look at these hands, supposing that partner has opened 1♠.

(a) ♠105	(b) ♠Q85	(c) ♠J2
♡KJ6	♡Q642	♡AJ8
◇KJ53	◇J9	◇K105
♣K1092	♣AQ92	♣Q7652

Hand (a) is well suited to an immediate 2NT response. You have good stoppers everywhere ('a dog in every kennel', as some players say) and only two cards in partner's suit. On (b) you have weak diamonds and three spades to an honour. Respond 2♣, intending to call 3♠ on the next round. A 2♣ response would be acceptable also on (c), but 2NT is preferable. It gives less information to the defenders.

When to respond 3NT

A direct leap to 3NT consumes an extravagant amount of bidding space, leaving partner little room in which to manoeuvre. Over one of a major suit such a response passes precise information: 13–15 points and a 4–3–3–3 distribution. Look at these hands:

(a) ♠K 104 (b) ♠J 93
   ♡Q 92   ♡A Q 62
   ◇A J 102   ◇J 65
   ♣Q J 3   ♣A Q 4

On (a) respond 3NT to 1♡ or 1♠. If partner's opening bid was based on a 5-card suit he can choose where to play, knowing that you have 3-card support. Hand (b) has a weak holding in diamonds and the best response to 1♠ is 2♣, rather than 3NT. This will give partner the chance to introduce a heart suit or to rebid his spades. An initial response of 2♡, remember, would suggest five cards in the suit.

Opposite a minor-suit opening the 3NT response covers a wider range of hands. Suppose that partner opens 1♣ and you hold either of these hands:

(a) ♠A Q 2 (b) ♠K 5
   ♡K 105   ♡K 82
   ◇Q 982   ◇J 92
   ♣K 43   ♣A Q 1072

You could reply 1◇ on (a) but where would this lead? A response of 3NT describes your hand well and takes you directly to the most likely final contract. 3NT is the most practical response on (b), too. The hand is much too strong for a raise to 3♣, which would be a non-forcing limit bid.

(b)   The Hold-up in Notrumps

When you are playing a notrump contract it is often right to hold up
your stopper in the suit led. The intention is to exhaust one of the
opponents of the suit. See how it works on this typical 3NT contract.

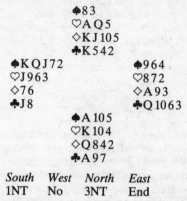

	♠83	
	♡AQ5	
	◇KJ105	
	♣K542	
♠KQJ72		♠964
♡J963		♡872
◇76		◇A93
♣J8		♣Q1063
	♠A105	
	♡K104	
	◇Q842	
	♣A97	

South	West	North	East
1NT	No	3NT	End

West leads ♠K, the top of his sequence. You can see what will
happen if you win the first or second round of spades. When East gains
the lead with ◇A he will have a spade to return. The defenders will
claim four spades and the diamond ace to put the contract one down.

Declarer should, of course, hold up ♠A until the third round,
exhausting East of the suit. He can then knock out ◇A with impunity.

Playing into the safe hand

Once a particular defender is out of the dangerous suit you can afford to
let him gain the lead. This may determine which of two suits you should
develop, as on the following deal:

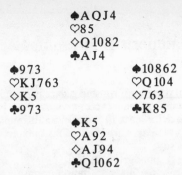

♠AQJ4
♡85
◇Q1082
♣AJ4

♠973   ♠10862
♡KJ763   ♡Q104
◇K5   ◇763
♣973   ♣K85

♠K5
♡A92
◇AJ94
♣Q1062

You reach 3NT on the South cards and West leads ♡6 to his partner's queen. You hold up ♡A until the third round, exhausting East of the suit. What should you play next? A diamond finesse would be dangerous. If it lost, West would quickly cash two hearts. The right move is to run ♣Q, finessing into the **safe hand**. The finesse loses, but the contract is safe. Declarer rises with the ace on the diamond return and claims nine tricks.

Holding up with a double stopper

When you have two cards to knock out before you can clear enough tricks for the contract, it may be necessary to hold up even when you have two stoppers in the opponents' suit. This type of deal is common:

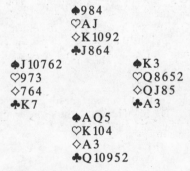

♠984
♡AJ
◇K1092
♣J864

♠J10762   ♠K3
♡973   ♡Q8652
◇764   ◇QJ85
♣K7   ♣A3

♠AQ5
♡K104
◇A3
♣Q10952

You play in 3NT from the South seat and West leads ♠6 to his partner's king. If you take the first trick and play on clubs East will win the first round and clear the spade suit. When West wins the next round of clubs he will meanly cash his long spades, putting you one down.

To make the contract you must duck the first round of spades. You win the next round and play on clubs. Since East has no spade to return, the suit can be safely established, giving you an easy nine tricks.

Day Eight
(a) The Opener's Rebid

When the auction starts with two suit bids, say 1◇ – 1♠, neither player
has a clear picture of his partner's strength. The opener's rebid
continues the search for a trump fit and gives an approximate idea of the
strength of his hand. These are the options open to him:

(a) to rebid his suit;
(b) to raise the responder's suit;
(c) to pass or raise partner's notrump response;
(d) to rebid in notrumps;
(e) to bid a new suit.

The opener rebids his suit

Suppose you have opened 1◇, non-vulnerable, and your partner has
responded 1♡. What should you rebid on these hands?

(a) ♠J104	(b) ♠Q95	(c) ♠AQ4
♡Q4	♡8	♡65
◇AQJ932	◇AKJ1082	◇KQ1095
♣K5	♣AQ2	♣A106

The first hand is a minimum opening bid, well suited to a 2◇ rebid.
Hand (b) is considerably stronger, worth a 3◇ rebid. Such a jump rebid
is non-forcing, facing a one-level response; it suggests around 16–18
points and a good 6-card suit. The final hand does contain a rebiddable
diamond suit, but the most accurate rebid is 1NT. You will recall that
this rebid shows 15–16 points when non-vulnerable.

The opener raises partner's suit

When the opener has 4-card support for his partner's major suit he will
make a **limit raise**. The higher he bids, the stronger his hand. After 1◇ –
1♠, how would you rebid on these hands?

(a) ♠A1082	(b) ♠KQ92	(c) ♠AKJ4
♡94	♡K63	♡Q6
◇AQJ74	◇AK1054	◇AKQ74
♣Q7	♣9	♣103

On (a) you rebid 2♠, indicating limited strength. Hand (b) is worth a
jump to 3♠, non-forcing, but showing good values. Hand (c), with 19
points facing a presumed 6 or so, is worth a 4♠ call.

When partner responds in notrumps

The response of 1NT, you will recall, suggests about 6–9 points. *Pass on
a balanced 16*, raise to 2NT on 17–18, to 3NT on 19–20. On unbalanced

hands remember that partner may be quite weak. After 1♡ –1NT, the opener holds:

(a) ♠A 102   (b) ♠7
   ♡AQJ962   ♡AKJ105
   ◇4   ◇AQ1072
   ♣A94   ♣K5

Rebid 3♡ on (a), strongly invitational but non-forcing. On (b) you say 3◇, forcing for one round.

The opener rebids in notrumps

We have already discussed the 1NT rebid. Jump rebids in notrumps indicate upwards of 17 points. This is a fair assessment:

1♡ – 1♠ – 2NT   the opener shows 17–18 points
1♣ – 1♠ – 3NT   the opener shows 19–20 points
1♡ – 2◇ – 2NT   the opener shows 15–16 points
1♠ – 2♣ – 3NT   the opener shows 17–18 points

The opener rebids a new suit

Finally, the opener may introduce a new suit. Suppose the auction has started 1◇ – 1♡ and you have to find a rebid on one of these hands:

(a) ♠AQ93   (b) ♠AK84   (c) ♠KQJ4
   ♡103   ♡5   ♡A5
   ◇KQJ64   ◇AQJ74   ◇AKQ105
   ♣84   ♣K102   ♣103

On (a) you rebid 1♠, non-forcing. You make the same rebid on (b), which is five points stronger. Hand (c), though, is too strong for a non-forcing rebid of 1♠. Bid 2♠, which is forcing to game.

Making a 'reverse' bid

When the opener rebids at the two-level in a suit that is higher than the one he opened he will be fairly strong, usually 16 upwards. Look at these two sequences:

(a) 1♡ 1♠ (b) 1◇ 1♠
   2◇   2♡

In the first sequence the responder can give preference to the opener's first, and normally longer, suit *at the same level*. In the second sequence the responder would have to bid 3◇ to give preference to the opener's main suit. Since the opener risks driving the bidding to the three-level even when partner holds minimum values, he must hold good values himself.

(b)   Which Suit to Play On

When you are playing in notrumps and need to establish tricks in more than one suit, it can be important to attack the right suit first. Deals like this are frequent:

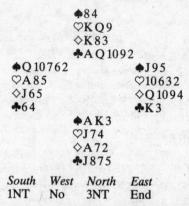

```
                    ♠84
                    ♡KQ9
                    ◇K83
                    ♣AQ1092
        ♠Q10762              ♠J95
        ♡A85                 ♡10632
        ◇J65                 ◇Q1094
        ♣64                  ♣K3
                    ♠AK3
                    ♡J74
                    ◇A72
                    ♣J875
```

South	West	North	East
1NT	No	3NT	End

West leads ♣6 and you win East's jack with the king. You can see what will happen if you take the club finesse at trick 2. East will win and clear the spade suit. You can hold up your second spade honour until the third round, but this will do you no good. Eventually you will have to play on hearts for your ninth trick. Since West has ♡A, along with two spade winners, you will go one down.

It is better at trick 2 to play on hearts, knocking out the potential entry to the danger hand (West, with the long spades). What can West do? If he wins with ♡A and reverts to spades, you will hold off the ace until the third round. It will then be safe to take the club finesse. If it loses and East has a spade left, the suit will have broken 4–4. You will therefore lose at most two spades, a heart and a club.

When the stoppers to be knocked out are both aces, declarer may have to guess which ace is held by the danger hand and must therefore be knocked out first. Declarer on the hand below claimed that he had been unlucky.

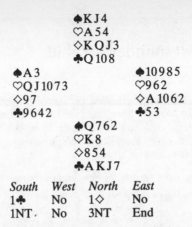

```
              ♠KJ4
              ♡A54
              ◇KQJ3
              ♣Q108
    ♠A3                    ♠10985
    ♡QJ1073                ♡962
    ◇97                    ◇A1062
    ♣9642                  ♣53
              ♠Q762
              ♡K8
              ◇854
              ♣AKJ7
```

South	West	North	East
1♣	No	1◇	No
1NT	No	3NT	End

West led ♡Q against 3NT. Declarer ducked the first round and took the second with the king. It seemed a complete guess whether he should play first on spades or diamonds. He decided to try a diamond. East won immediately and cleared the heart suit. When the diamonds refused to divide 3–3, declarer had to play on spades. West won with the ace and cashed two heart winners, putting the game one down.

'My usual luck,' South complained. 'If I guess to play on spades I make it.'

In fact on this particular deal declarer does not need to guess which ace West holds. After winning with ♡K he should cross to ♣Q and lead ♠4 towards his queen. As it happens, West holds ♠A. He wins and clears the hearts, but since East has no hearts left when the diamond ace is dislodged the contract is secure. (If West does not take ♠A on the first round, South switches to diamonds.)

What would happen if the two aces were reversed, though, East holding ♠A? If East played ♠A on thin air when dummy's ♠4 was led, declarer would have three spade tricks, enough for the contract. If instead East ducked, declarer would be able to win with ♠Q and turn to diamonds with one spade trick in the bag.

Playing the contract in this fashion, declarer ensures the contract unless West holds five hearts to the queen-jack and both the missing aces. This is extremely unlikely since he did not overcall 1♡ on the first round of bidding.

Day Nine
(a) The Responder's Rebid

The opener has already given some picture of his strength by the time the responder has to make his second call. The responder's task usually is to add his own strength to that indicated by his partner and to decide whether a game contract is unlikely, still possible, or certain. We shall look at these three cases in turn.

Game is unlikely – the responder does not encourage

Suppose that the bidding has started like this:

West	East
1♡	1♠
2♢	?

As East, there are three weak calls you can make to tell your partner that game is unlikely from your point of view. You can pass, return to opener's first suit at the minimum level (here 2♡), or rebid your own suit at the minimum level (here 2♠). These three hands all qualify for limited action:

(a) ♠AJ84   (b) ♠A10752   (c) ♠A109654
    ♡64   ♡103   ♡7
    ♢J962   ♢J2   ♢1043
    ♣1082   ♣Q942   ♣K62

You pass on (a); you have some diamond support, but insufficient values to suggest a game in diamonds or notrumps. On (b) you should bid 2♡, **giving preference** to partner's first suit. You may find this call rather strange, but remember that partner is likely to have more hearts than diamonds. You are merely correcting the contract from a possible 4–2 fit to a likely 5–2 fit. On (c) you might consider passing, but it is better to rebid 2♠, again a limited call.

When the opener's second call was at the one level the responder has other weakish rebids at his disposal. Say that the bidding has begun:

West	East
1♣	1♡
1♠	?

... and as East you hold:

(a) ♠93   (b) ♠K1054
    ♡K10952   ♡A962
    ♢AJ82   ♢852
    ♣72   ♣93

On (a) you bid 1NT, suggesting about 7–10 points. With (b) you raise to 2♠, just as you would if partner had opened 1♠.

Game is possible – the responder invites

When the responder has around 10–12 points, or corresponding distributional values, he may wish to invite a game contract. Suppose the bidding has started like this:

West	East
1◇	1♡
2♣	?

These are some typical hands for responder:

(a) ♠AJ9	(b) ♠9653	(c) ♠A2
♡AQ65	♡KJ104	♡AQ10762
◇J43	◇AQ92	◇964
♣952	♣6	♣103

Hand (a), with a secure spade stopper and 12 points, is typical of a 2NT rebid. On (b) you would give jump preference to 3◇. Hand (c) is too strong for a minimum 2♡; it is worth 3♡, a strong invitation to game.

Responder wants to play in game

When the responder holds an opening bid himself, or an excellent fit with one of partner's suits, he will normally be worth a game call at his second turn. Suppose that the bidding has begun:

West	East
1♠	2◇
2♡	?

... and as East you hold one of these hands:

(a) ♠A1073	(b) ♠6	(c) ♠8
♡K4	♡AQ62	♡Q42
◇AQ962	◇AQJ94	◇AJ1072
♣63	♣1073	♣KQJ9

On (a) you would rebid 4♠ (remember that 3♠ would be non-forcing). On (b) you would raise to 4♡ and on (c) you would bid 3NT.

(b)   The Rule of Eleven

When the opening lead is 'fourth best', both the defender in the third seat and declarer can make use of a mathematical calculation known as the **Rule of Eleven**. It is most easily understood by looking at an example. Suppose the suit opened lies like this:

$$\heartsuit A Q 4$$
$$\heartsuit J 8 7 6 \qquad \qquad \heartsuit K 10 9 3$$
$$\heartsuit 5 2$$

West leads ♡6. The rule says: **Subtract the spot-card led from 11 and that will tell you how many cards higher than the one led the other three players hold**. Here East will subtract 6 from 11, deducing that North, East and South hold between them five cards higher than the 6. Since he has three of them and dummy has the other two, declarer cannot beat the 6. If declarer plays low from dummy, East will follow with the 3, allowing West to attack dummy's tenace again.

East made good use of the rule on this deal:

```
                    ♠542
                    ♡AQ82
                    ◇J106
                    ♣KQ7
     ♠K9863                      ♠QJ7
     ♡764                        ♡1095
     ◇97                         ◇A54
     ♣J82                        ♣9643
                    ♠A10
                    ♡KJ3
                    ◇KQ832
                    ♣A105
```

South	West	North	East
1NT	No	3NT	End

West led ♣6 and East's jack was taken by declarer's ace. Declarer had eight top tricks and needed to slip through a diamond trick to bring his total to nine. He crossed to ♣K and led ◇J from dummy, trying to look like a man with ◇K9xx, about to take a finesse.

East was not taken in by this ruse. He went up with the ace and played queen and another spade, sinking the contract. How was he able to read the position so well, do you think? After the first trick he knew that declarer had only one spade higher than the 6 left in his hand (he had started with two, according to the Rule of 11). Declarer's remaining spade could not be the king because West would not have led low from a holding headed by the 1098. Also, it was likely that South had started with only two spades. With three, he would doubtless have held up the ace for two rounds, hoping to break the link between the two defenders.

Sometimes the third player can use the rule to gauge that partner has *not* led fourth best from a good suit. This kind of deduction helped East to beat 3NT on the following hand:

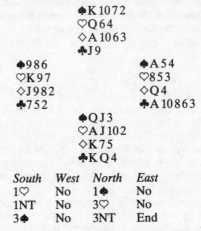

South	West	North	East
1♡	No	1♠	No
1NT	No	3♡	No
3♠	No	3NT	End

West made the happy lead of ♣7. Since East could see five clubs higher than the 7, he realized that his partner's card must be a top-of-nothing lead. He therefore played the 8 at trick one, an encouraging signal. When declarer knocked out ♠A, East returned a low club, retaining his ace as a subsequent re-entry. Declarer won, cashed the spade suit and continued with a heart finesse, which lost to West's king. The defenders could now cash three club tricks to put the game one down.

Declarer, too, may take advantage of the rule:

                    ♠AQJ2
    ♠K10864   ♠5
                    ♠973

West leads ♠6 against a notrump contract.
Declarer can see five cards higher than the 6 in his own hand and dummy. He knows therefore that East cannot beat the 6. He runs the opening lead to his 9, scoring four tricks in the suit.

Day Ten
(a) Fourth Suit Forcing

In the section on the responder's rebid we noted that whenever responder raises one of his partner's suits or rebids his own suit, this is always a limit bid. When the responder's hand is too strong for a limit bid on the second round and is unsuitable also for a direct game bid, he may find himself in a quandary. Say that the bidding has started like this:

West	West	East
♠AQJ52		1♡
♡K3	1♠	2◇
◇A63	?	
♣742		

What can you say on the West cards? You want to be in game, but calls of 3◇, 3♡ and 3♠ would all be non-forcing limit bids. You don't want to plunge into 4♡, 4♠ or 5◇; still less can you contemplate 3NT with no guard in clubs, the unbid suit.

There is an ingenious solution to bidding problems of this type. You bid the **fourth suit**, here 3♣. This does not show a club suit; if you had values in clubs you would doubtless be bidding notrumps now. **A bid of the fourth suit is a forward move implying that you may not be quite certain which way to go**. It asks the opener to continue describing his hand.

Here is another use of the bid:

West	West	East
♠KJ852		1♡
♡102	1♠	2♣
◇A9	?	
♣AQ74		

If West raises directly to 3♣, this would be a non-forcing limit bid. He therefore makes a fourth-suit-forcing bid of 2◇, intending to follow this with 3♣, which would then become forcing.

To what level is a fourth-suit call forcing?

A bid in the fourth suit is forcing to game at the three level, but not at the two level. Say that the bidding has started:

West	East
1◇	1♠
2♣	2♡
?	

What should West say next on these two hands:

(a) ♠Q6   (b) ♠Q83
    ♡92   ♡84
    ◇AK764   ◇A10973
    ♣A1083   ♣AK72

On (a) you bid just 2♠, non-forcing. East is very likely to have five spades, so this will be a comfortable resting-place if he passes. Hand (b) will play powerfully in a spade contract. You are well worth a call of 3♠ at this stage.

This situation is similar:

West   East
1◇   1♠
2♣   2♡
?

What should you say on these West hands:

(a) ♠6   (b) ♠7
    ♡KJ7   ♡A109
    ◇AQ982   ◇AK1054
    ♣Q1052   ♣KJ43

On (a) you call 2NT, which your partner is allowed to pass. You have 15 points on (b), which puts you in the game zone; partner should have fair values – not less than 10 points on this sequence. Your call now is 3NT.

When responding to a fourth-suit call the general rule is: two level bids are non-forcing; three-level bids are forcing to game.

(b)   Blocking the Defenders' Suit

When you are playing in notrumps we have already seen how effective it can be to hold up the ace of the defenders' main suit. Sometimes, though, you can block the defenders' suit by playing the ace on the first round. Look at this deal:

```
                        ♠J73
                        ♡KQ72
                        ◇A2
                        ♣KQ42
        ♠962                        ♠Q1085
        ♡65                         ♡J10984
        ◇KJ874                      ◇Q10
        ♣A93                        ♣76
                        ♠AK4
                        ♡A3
                        ◇9653
                        ♣J1085
```

South	West	North	East
		1♡	No
2NT	No	3NT	End

West led ◇7 and declarer saw that the only threat to the contract was that the diamonds were 5–2 and West held ♣A. What if West did hold five diamonds? Declarer applied the Rule of Eleven: 7 from 11 was 4. He could see only two cards higher than the 7, so East's doubleton must include two more. Since West would have led an honour from combinations such as KQJ, QJ10, KJ10 and KQ10, it followed that East's cards were both higher than the 9. Declarer therefore played ◇A at trick 1, confident that this would block the defenders' suit. He forced out ♣A immediately and the defenders were unable to cash their diamond tricks. After the first trick the suit lay like this:

```
                ◇2
        ◇KJ84           ◇Q
                ◇965
```

Had declarer held off ◇A for one round the contract would have gone down.

Here is a similar position:

```
                ♡A73
        ♡K10862         ♡Q9
                ♡J54
```

40

West leads ♡6. If West may hold the critical entry and you judge that East has a heart honour (which is likely), you rise with dummy's ace on the first round.

Another common situation where declarer can block the defenders' suit is when the opening lead is from three to an honour. This deal is typical:

```
                    ♠ A K 4
                    ♡ 7 5
                    ◇ K Q 10 9 3
                    ♣ K 6 3
  ♠ J 9 6 2                        ♠ 8 7 5
  ♡ Q 8 2                          ♡ A 10 9 6 4
  ◇ 7 6 5                          ◇ A 2
  ♣ 10 8 5                         ♣ Q J 4
                    ♠ Q 10 3
                    ♡ K J 3
                    ◇ J 8 4
                    ♣ A 9 7 2
```

South	West	North	East
		1◇	1♡
2NT	No	3NT	End

West started with ♡2, won by East's ace. Back came ♡10. West's lead of a low card, the 2, suggested that he held an honour. This had to be the queen. Declarer saw that he could block the hearts by playing his king on the second round. West followed with the 8, leaving the heart suit like this:

```
            ♡ —
  ♡ Q               ♡ 9 6 4
            ♡ J
```

Declarer now knocked out ◇A. There was nothing the defenders could do. West's ♡Q won the last trick for his side.

Day Eleven
(a) Heading for 3NT

Three notrumps is the most common game contract, mainly because it requires the fewest tricks. Even when you have a good fit in a minor suit, it will usually be easier to score nine tricks in notrumps than eleven in the suit.

When a notrump game is being contemplated it is sometimes convenient to make bids known as 'notrump probes'. These show values in the suit bid, but do not guarantee a 4-card suit. Here are some examples:

West	East	West	East
♠106	♠AJ4	1◇	1♡
♡Q2	♡AJ854	3◇	3♠
◇AKJ1096	◇732	3NT	
♣AQ4	♣102		

When East hears a jump rebid from West he knows that the partnership has the values for game. His bid of 3♠ shows values in spades, but not necessarily four cards there. East can hardly be looking for a spade fit, since West would doubtless have rebid 1♠ if he held a fair suit of spades. West has a healthy stop in clubs, so he is happy to bid 3NT.

Here responder makes a stop-showing bid after a fit has been found in a minor suit:

West	East	West	East
♠KQ4	♠J2	1♡	2♣
♡AQ762	♡94	3♣	3◇
◇5	◇KJ8	3NT	
♣K542	♣AQ10976		

East is too strong to pass 3♣ and it would be an undisciplined gamble to bid 3NT with only J x in spades. He bids 3◇, showing no more than a stop in the suit.

When the opponents have bid a suit

When the opponents have shown a good suit by overcalling you may need special measures to determine whether game in notrumps is a possibility. The general idea is to bid notrumps if you have their suit stopped. When you have a strong hand but no stop in their suit, you make a cue bid. Suppose the auction has started like this:

South	West	North	East
			1◇
1♡	1♠	No	3◇
No	?		

You might hold one of these hands as West:

(a) ♠A Q 7 3 2 (b) ♠K Q 10 6 4
   ♡A 10 4   ♡8 2
   ◇9 2   ◇K 7 4
   ♣J 6 3   ♣Q 10 5

No problem on (a). With a sound stop in hearts, the opponents' suit, you call 3NT. Hand (b) contains the values for game, facing a jump rebid, but you have no heart stop. Bid 3♡, a cue bid in the opponents' suit. If East has a heart stop himself he can call 3NT. Failing that, he may be able to support your spades.

Note that when you do hold a stopper in the enemy suit you should incline to 3NT, even though you may not hold a secure guard in the unbid suit.

When the opponents have bid two suits

What if the opponents have bid two suits? Now a cue bid in one of their suits will show a stop in that suit, but not in the other suit.

Imagine this is the auction so far:

South	West	North	East
1♡	1♠	2♣	2◇
No	No	?	

You hold one of these North hands:

(a) ♠K J 4   (b) ♠10 3
   ♡9 5   ♡K 6
   ◇8 3   ◇A J 4
   ♣A K J 8 5 2 ♣K Q 10 8 4 2

Bid 2♠ on (a), 3◇ on (b).

(b)   Safety Play

There is a right and a wrong way to tackle most suit combinations. Suppose you need five tricks from this suit:

North
A K 9 5 2

South
Q 8 6 3

If the suit divides 2–2 or 3–1 there will be no problem. What if one defender holds J 10 x x? If it is East you cannot deny him a trick. You can pick up all four cards with West, though, provided you start by playing the *queen*. If East shows out on the first round you can subsequently lead twice towards the North hand, covering whatever cards West plays.

Sometimes the best play in a suit depends on how many tricks you need from it.

North
A Q 10 8 2

South
7 6 5 3

If you cannot afford to lose a trick you finesse the queen on the first round. Unless the jack appears from East (in which case you will finesse the 10 next), you cash the ace on the second round. You make all five tricks when West has K x, also when East has a singleton jack and West K x x.

Suppose you can afford to lose one trick but not two. Then you do better to cash the ace on the first round. You then lead towards North's Q–10, covering West's card. This will save you two losers when East has a singleton king.

The same principle applies with this combination:

North
K J 6 2

South
A 9 5 3

If you cannot afford a loser you finesse the jack on the first round. You will pick up the suit when West has Q x x, Q x or a singleton queen. If you can afford one loser, you cash the king on the first round, then lead low towards the South hand. If East follows with a small card, you finesse the 9; if East shows out on the second round, you rise with the ace and lead back towards the jack. This restricts your losers to one when either defender holds Q 10 x x.

We have looked at the above suit combinations in isolation. There are many others of a similar kind. Often your play in one suit will be affected by some grander strategy.

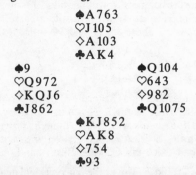

♠A763
♡J105
♢A103
♣AK4

♠9
♡Q972
♢KQJ6
♣J862

♠Q104
♡643
♢982
♣Q1075

♠KJ852
♡AK8
♢754
♣93

South arrives in four spades and West attacks in diamonds. Declarer sees that the contract is safe unless he loses a trick in both hearts and spades. His plan is to cash ♠A and finesse ♠J, having previously made sure that if this loses to a doubleton spade queen West will have to surrender a trick on his return.

Declarer wins the second round of diamonds, cashes ♣A K and ruffs a club. He then crosses to ♠A and finesses ♠J. As it happens, the finesse succeeds, giving him an easy ten tricks. Had the finesse lost, West would have had no safe return after cashing the third round of diamonds. A heart would obviously be fatal and a fourth club or diamond would allow declarer to ruff in one hand and discard a heart loser from the other.

Day Twelve
(a) The Two Club Opening

An opening bid of 2♣ is a conventional call promising a very strong hand. If the hand is balanced it will contain 23 points or more. If it is unbalanced the playing strength will justify a game contract however weak partner may be. These are typical 2♣ openings:

(a) ♠AQ9   (b) ♠AK103
    ♡AK104   ♡KJ4
    ◇KJ4   ◇AQ
    ♣AQ6   ♣AKJ5

(c) ♠AKQ92   (d) ♠AK
    ♡K2   ♡A
    ◇AKQ54   ◇AJ4
    ♣6   ♣KQJ10972

On (a) you will rebid 2NT over the conventional negative response of 2◇. This is a non-forcing rebid announcing 23–24 points. Any rebid except 2NT is forcing to game. On (b), with 25 points, the rebid is 3NT. On (c) you will rebid 2♠, intending to show your diamonds on the next round. On (d) your rebid will be 3♣.

As you see from the sample hands above, a 2♣ opening guarantees a fair measure of high cards, usually at least 20 points. Hands with fewer points should not be opened 2♣, however powerful they may be in terms of playing strength. Look at these two healthy specimens:

(a) ♠AKQJ10972 (b) ♠—
    ♡J8   ♡KQJ1082
    ◇—   ◇AQ10985
    ♣AJ2   ♣6

You want to be in game on either of these hands, but neither is ideal for a 2♣ opening. They contain too few quick tricks, too little defence. Such hands should be opened with an Acol Two bid – 2♠ on (a), 2♡ on (b). We will look at these calls on Day Thirteen.

Responding to two clubs

The most common response to 2♣ is 2◇, keeping the bidding low and waiting to hear what type of hand partner has. If instead you respond with a suit call at the minimum level (3◇ with a diamond suit), this will show around 8 points or more and a suit worth mentioning. A response of 2NT shows a flat hand with similar values. These are typical auctions:

West	East	West	East
♠AQ6	♠KJ842	2♣	2◇
♡A5	♡1082	2NT[1]	3♠[2]
◇AKJ4	◇72	4♠[3]	
♣KQJ2	♣973		

[1] 23–24 points over here, partner.

[2] I have enough for game at least and five or more spades.

[3] Spades sound a better prospect than notrumps in that case.

Note that it would be quite wrong for West to bid anything more than 4♠. He has already shown an excellent hand and must leave to his partner any move towards a slam. He must not bid the same values twice.

When responder has useful values it is his responsibility to show them:

West	East	West	East
♠A5	♠9762	2♣	2◇
♡AKJ1082	♡Q5	2♡	2NT
◇AJ	◇KQ6	4♡	5♡
♣AK3	♣10842	6♡	

West was willing to play in four hearts with a worthless hand opposite. Since East's hand is likely to contribute at least two tricks to a heart contract he should not let the bidding die in game.

Now a couple of auctions where East makes a positive response:

West	East	West	East
♠KJ84	♠AQ7	2♣	2NT[1]
♡AQ	♡1054	6NT[2]	
◇AQ5	◇K983		
♣AKQ6	♣852		

[1] Balanced hand of 8 or more points here, partner.

[2] Excellent! With at least 33 points between the two hands, 6NT should be on.

West	East	West	East
♠82	♠AK1052	2♣	2♠[1]
♡AKQ1062	♡J5	3♡[2]	4♡[3]
◇AK3	◇1084	6♡	
♣AK	♣J76		

[1] I have 8 points or more and a fair spade suit.

[2] My opening was based on a strong heart suit, partner.

[3] In that case my Jx should be good enough support.

(b)   Counting the Defenders' Points

When you are playing the dummy you can often make use of
information gained during the auction. If one of the defenders opened
the bidding it is reasonable to place him with at least 12 points. If his
partner failed to respond to the opening bid he is unlikely to hold as
many as 6 points. Declarer drew such an inference on this deal:

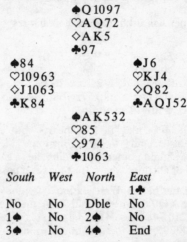

```
                    ♠Q1097
                    ♡AQ72
                    ◇AK5
                    ♣97
    ♠84                         ♠J6
    ♡10963                      ♡KJ4
    ◇J1063                      ◇Q82
    ♣K84                        ♣AQJ52
                    ♠AK532
                    ♡85
                    ◇974
                    ♣1063
```

South	West	North	East
			1♣
No	No	Dble	No
1♠	No	2♠	No
3♠	No	4♠	End

South eventually reached four spades and the defenders started with
a club to the ace and ♣Q return. West overtook with the king and
switched to a heart. It might seem to an unthinking player that the
contract depended on the heart finesse. West has already shown up with
♣K, though, and with ♡K as well he would doubtless have responded
to his partner's opening. Declarer therefore went up with ♡A, drew
trumps, then ducked a second round of hearts. The king of hearts fell
when he ruffed a third round of the suit and he was able to discard his
diamond loser on ♡Q.

Similar inferences will sometimes save you a crucial guess. Look at
this deal:

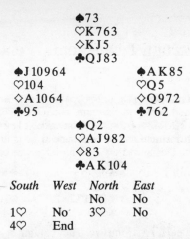

```
              ♠73
              ♡K763
              ◇KJ5
              ♣QJ83
♠J10964                    ♠AK85
♡104                       ♡Q5
◇A1064                     ◇Q972
♣95                        ♣762
              ♠Q2
              ♡AJ982
              ◇83
              ♣AK104
```

South	West	North	East
		No	No
1♡	No	3♡	No
4♡	End		

West started with ♣J and his partner cashed two rounds of the suit.
Declarer won the club switch and drew trumps in two rounds. It seemed
that the contract would depend on a successful diamond guess, but
declarer recalled that East had been unable to open the bidding. He had
already shown 9 points in the majors and would surely have opened the
bidding if he had held ◇A as well. Placing the diamond ace with West,
declarer led a diamond and rose with dummy's king. Ten tricks
resulted.

Suppose that the bidding had started differently, East opening a
12–14 notrump. Now declarer would draw the opposite conclusion.
Realizing that East needed ◇A to make up his opening bid, he would
be more inclined to finesse the jack of diamonds.

Day Thirteen
(a) The Strong Two Bid

We have already looked at the 2♣ opening, the first thrust on most hands where you expect to reach game however weak partner may be. Opening bids of 2◇, 2♡ and 2♠ are strong also. They indicate a hand of **power and quality**, including at least one good suit. Consider these hands:

(a) ♠AKQ1082   (b) ♠A5   (c) ♠KQJ62
     ♡AQ5   ♡K5   ♡AKJ53
     ◇A   ◇KQJ10752   ◇A7
     ♣J95   ♣A3   ♣8

All three are ideal for a strong two. They contain at least eight playing tricks and a fair measure of defensive strength. Open 2♠ on (a), 2◇ on (b), 2♠ on (c). Strong-two openings are forcing for one round.

These hands are *not* suitable for such action:

(a) ♠AQ7652   (b) ♠85
     ♡K5   ♡AKQJ1084
     ◇AJ   ◇9
     ♣A92   ♣KQ2

When you are considering a strong two bid ask yourself 'If I open with a one bid and this is passed out, will I risk missing a game?' If the answer is 'No', prefer the one bid. Apply this test to hand (a). It is most unlikely that you will miss a game by opening 1♠. If partner cannot find a 1NT response even nine tricks are a long way off.

Hand (b) does contain the necessary playing strength for a two bid, but it is hardly a 'hand of quality'. Open 1♡, intending to bid strongly at your next turn. (In third or fourth position you could open 4♡.)

Strong with clubs?

When you have a powerful hand based on a good club suit, there is no strong two bid available. You must therefore choose between a top-heavy 1♣ and a lightweight 2♣. These are borderline hands:

(a) ♠K105   (b) ♠4
     ♡A9   ♡KQ2
     ◇A7   ◇AK
     ♣AKJ1062   ♣AQJ9762

Both hands would be worthy of a strong two if the long suit were anything but clubs. My vote would be to open 2♣ on (a) where there is likely to be some play for 3NT however weak partner may be. On (b) you cannot make game unless you find partner with one good card. Risk a modest 1♣; it is unlikely to be passed out.

Responding to a strong two bid

On weak hands you make a negative response of 2NT. The bidding may then stop in three of the suit that was opened. To respond in a new suit shows around 8 points and a very fair suit. Imagine your partner has opened 2♠ and you hold one of these hands:

(a) ♠62   (b) ♠1054   (c) ♠82
     ♡J964   ♡J1073   ♡K5
     ◇974   ◇85   ◇KQJ102
     ♣J843   ♣K1042   ♣8754

On (a) you would respond 2NT, honouring your obligation to keep the bidding alive. Should partner rebid 3♠, you pass. Over a rebid of 3◇ correct to 3♠, non-forcing. Over 3♣ bid 4♣.

Hand (b) is considerably better than (a). You have three-card trump support, a doubleton and one high card. You would still respond 2NT, but after that you would carry the bidding to 4♠. Hand (c) represents the minimum on which you would give a positive response, here 3◇.

When you have positive values and trump support for partner you give a single raise. This response is forcing and may be the first move on a good hand. A raise directly to game, such as 2♡–4♡, traditionally expresses a fair hand with no ace. Say that partner has opened 2♡ and you hold one of these hands:

(a) ♠64   (b) ♠853   (c) ♠Q9
     ♡K105   ♡QJ54   ♡Q1064
     ◇AJ62   ◇K1082   ◇92
     ♣9764   ♣Q2   ♣AKJ54

Hand (a) contains good trump support and an ace. Give partner the good news by raising to 3♡. On (b) raise directly to 4♡, showing fair values but no ace. With hand (c) you have your sights on a slam. To paint the picture respond 3♣ rather than 3♡. You can support the hearts enthusiastically on the next round.

(b) Declarer's Communications

There are various clever plays you can make when entries to dummy are scarce. Suppose you are playing in a notrump contract and you have a suit like this:

> *North*
> A762
>
> *South*
> KQJ5

If both defenders follow to the king and queen you can play the jack to the ace on the third round. At some later stage you can lead the 5 to the 7, gaining a second entry to the North hand.

Declarer used such a technique on this deal:

```
                    ♠Q52
                    ♡1084
                    ◇AK93
                    ♣762
    ♠J10983                    ♠K64
    ♡Q9532                     ♡K76
    ◇65                        ◇842
    ♣4                         ♣K985
                    ♠A7
                    ♡AJ
                    ◇QJ107
                    ♣AQJ103
```

South arrived in six diamonds and West decided to try his luck with ♠J rather than the singleton club. Without much hope declarer played dummy's queen. Sure enough it was headed by the king, won by South's ace.

To make the contract now South needed five club tricks. He would then be able to discard two spades from dummy and ruff a spade for his twelfth trick. At trick 2 he played ◇Q, overtaken by dummy's ace. A finesse of ♣Q was successful and declarer continued with ◇J to dummy's king. When West showed out on a second club finesse and was unable to ruff, declarer saw that his care in the trump suit would be rewarded. He crossed to dummy for the third time by leading ◇7 to the 9. Another club finesse set up the suit and he proceeded to discard two spades (or hearts) on his ♣A3. Then a ruff in dummy produced a well-earned twelve tricks.

You can sometimes create an extra entry by taking an 'unnecessary' finesse. Suppose you have one of these holdings:

(a) ◇A Q 10   (b) ♡A 9

  ◇K 7 4   ♡K Q J 5 4

If West holds ◇J in (a) you can create three diamond entries to the North hand by finessing the 10 on the first round. In the second position you could finesse dummy's ♡9 if you needed an extra entry to dummy.

There is one type of hand where you deliberately surrender a trick in order to gain a valuable entry. Here is an example:

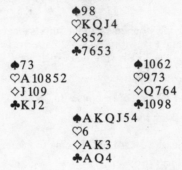

```
                    ♠98
                    ♡KQJ4
                    ◇852
                    ♣7653
  ♠73                         ♠1062
  ♡A10852                     ♡973
  ◇J109                       ◇Q764
  ♣KJ2                        ♣1098
                    ♠AKQJ54
                    ♡6
                    ◇AK3
                    ♣AQ4
```

You play in four spades and win the diamond lead. It is natural to try to slip through a heart at trick 2, but West, noting dummy's lack of entries, rises with the ace and continues with another diamond.

If you play in straightforward fashion now, drawing trumps, you will lose one heart, one diamond and two clubs. Instead you should lead a low trump towards dummy's 9 8 at trick 4. East wins with the 10, cashes a diamond trick and switches to a club. You rise with the ace, cross to ♠8 and discard two clubs on dummy's heart winners.

Even if dummy's trumps had been ♠9 2, you should still lead towards the 9, hoping that the 10 would be onside. This is a better proposition than playing the ace and 4 of clubs, hoping to find a doubleton king.

Day Fourteen
(a) Opening Bids of 2NT and 3NT

An opening call of 2NT shows a balanced hand of 20–22 points – this type of hand:

(a) ♠AQ102   (b) ♠KQ4   (c) ♠AQ92
    ♡KQ9   ♡AQ   ♡AKJ3
    ◇A105   ◇Q105   ◇J5
    ♣KQ4   ♣AQJ54   ♣AK5

Hand (a) with good stoppers in all the suits is ideal in every way for a 2NT call. So is hand (b), with a 5–3–3–2 pattern. The diamond suit is unguarded on (c), but 2NT is still the best choice.

Responding to 2NT

This is the general scheme of responses to 2NT:

3♣ Stayman, asking for 4-card majors.

3◇/3♡/3♠ At least a 5-card suit, forcing to game.

3NT/4♡/4♠ To play.

Let's look at some typical auctions.

(a) *West*   *East*   *West*   *East*
    ♠AQ5   ♠KJ962   2NT   3♠[1]
    ♡KQ105   ♡J3   4♠[2]   End
    ◇A6   ◇954
    ♣AQ94   ♣J83

[1]I have enough points for game and five or more spades.
[2]Better play in 4♠, then. My diamonds look a bit weak.

(b) *West*   *East*   *West*   *East*
    ♠AK5   ♠64   2NT   3♣[1]
    ♡AQ104   ♡K962   3♡[2]   4♡[3]
    ◇K63   ◇J85
    ♣AJ4   ♣Q1092

[1]Have you a 4-card major?
[2]Yes, in hearts.
[3]Just what I was looking for.

	(c) *West*	*East*	*West*	*East*
	♠AK104	♠QJ973	2NT	3♠[1]
	♡K1075	♡3	4♣[2]	4NT[3]
	◇AK6	◇Q1084	5♠[4]	6♠
	♣A3	♣KQ4		

[1]Enough points for game, partner, and 5 or more spades.

[2]I have a splendid fit for spades and a control in clubs.

[3]We may have enough values for a slam. I trust you have three aces (see Day Eighteen).

[4]I have indeed.

As you see in this last example, the opener should make a cue bid (here 4♣) when he has a good fit for the long suit shown by responder. We will look further at cue bids on Day Eighteen.

The Gambling 3NT Opening

Balanced hands of 23 points or more are covered by the 2♣ opening. The 3NT opening is used to show a solid 7-card minor suit with no more than a queen or so outside – this type of hand:

(a) ♠Q5	(b) ♠103
♡4	♡94
◇AKQJ1083	◇83
♣J93	♣AKQJ1094

Partner will pass 3NT only if he has sufficient outside stoppers himself. If he responds 4♣, this means he wants to play at the four level in your suit.

Say that partner opens 3NT and you hold this hand:

♠AKQJ
♡K94
◇3
♣AJ542

What would you say? There is only one good call – 6◇! Your partner has seven tricks in diamonds and you can add five more. By bidding the slam in diamonds, rather than notrumps, you protect ♡K from the opening lead.

(b)   The Opening Lead against Notrumps

The defenders' initial aim in most notrump contracts is to establish their own best suit. Unless your partner has indicated a suit during the auction you will normally start with your own longest suit. Say that the bidding has gone 1NT–3NT and you are on lead with one of these hands:

(a) ♠KJ972 (b) ♠83 (c) ♠K1083
  ♥A53   ♥KJ93   ♥Q6
  ♦Q2   ♦1074   ♦J92
  ♣964   ♣QJ105 ♣K1073

(a) ♠KJ972 (b) ♠83 (c) ♠K1083
  ♡A53 ♡KJ93 ♡Q6
  ◇Q2 ◇1074 ◇J92
  ♣964 ♣QJ105 ♣K1073

With (a) you will obviously attack in spades. If you strike gold and find your partner with the ace or queen you will be half-way to beating the contract. On (b) you have to choose between two 4-card suits. The sequence of honours makes a club lead more attractive. What should you do on (c), where you hold two suits of similar quality? Toss a coin? No, it is better to lead the major suit. There is a fair inference that the responder does *not* hold four spades, which might have induced him to bid a Stayman 2♣.

Which card should you lead?

Once you have decided which suit to lead, the usual choice of card is as follows:

(a) From a sequence of honours, such as A K Q or K Q J, lead the top card.

(b) From a 'broken sequence', such as A K J or K Q 10, again lead the top card.

(c) From an 'interior sequence', such as A Q J or K J 10, lead the middle honour.

(d) Otherwise lead fourth best from any suit containing an honour. Lead the 4 from Q974 or K10742. From three to an honour lead the bottom card, the 2 from Q82.

(e) From four small cards lead the second highest and follow with the bottom card on the next round. From 8643 lead the 6, then play the 3.

(f) From two or three small cards, lead the top one and follow with the next highest on the second round. Lead the 7 from 742, and play the 4 on the next round.

You can see the general idea when you lead a spot-card. A low one suggests a good suit, a high one a bad suit.

When the opponents have bid one or more suits

If the opponents bid some suits on the way to 3NT you will usually avoid leading one of them. Say that you have to find a lead after this auction:

South	West	North	East
1♠	No	2♣	No
2NT	No	3NT	End

What would you lead from these hands?

(a) ♠A Q 9 2   (b) ♠J 9
    ♡J 8 4   ♡7 6 5
    ♢10 9 2   ♢K 10 4
    ♣8 5 2   ♣Q 10 8 5 3

South has at least four spades on (a) so it would be silly to lead a spade. You should lead one of the unbid suits and the two touching cards in diamonds make ♢10 the more attractive proposition. On (b) you should again choose between the red suits. Prefer a heart because the opponents are less likely to hold concealed strength in a major than in a minor; also it may cost a trick to lead away from your diamond honours.

Leading from a worthless hand

The general purpose of leading from a long suit is to establish the low cards in it. There is little point in this unless you have some prospect of regaining the lead to cash the established cards. Say that the bidding has gone 1NT – 3NT: what would you lead from these hands?

(a) ♠J 7 4   (b) ♠7 6 5
    ♡9 8 2   ♡J 8 6 4
    ♢Q   ♢9 7 3
    ♣10 8 6 5 4 2   ♣J 5 2

There is no future in a club lead from (a). Even if partner holds a high honour in clubs the chance of establishing and running the suit is slim indeed. You should lead a major, but the choice is something of a guess. The ♡9 is safest, but the spade lead offers a better chance to establish a powerful attack. Partner might hold such as K Q x x x.

On (b) a heart lead will often give away a trick to no good effect. You should lead a spade or a diamond and the better choice is generally the major suit. Reach for ♠7.

Day Fifteen
(a) Pre-emptive Openings

An opening bid at the three level conventionally denotes a hand with fair playing strength but little defence. It is an obstructive manœuvre designed to make life awkward for the opponents, who may well hold the balance of the points. Look at these hands:

(a) ♠KQJ9765 (b) ♠K1098632 (c) ♠83
    ♡84   ♡5   ♡K4
    ◇J82   ◇AQ4   ◇92
    ♣6   ♣105   ♣KJ108762

Hand (a) is ideal for pre-emptive action; it contains six playing tricks and almost no defence. Traditionalists use the **Rule of 500** to gauge whether a hand is strong enough for a three bid. This means your hand should be strong enough on its own to make a penalty of more than 500 unlikely. The modern trend is to be bolder than this when the hand is particularly suitable for pre-emption. You should therefore open 3♠ on (a) even when vulnerable.

Hand (b) is not so suitable. It has less playing strength than (a), and the honours are not mostly in the long suit. Prefer an opening bid of 1♠ or even a pass. Hand (c) is worth a non-vulnerable 3♣ opening. Vulnerable, the call might prove expensive.

Your position at the table

Conditions are favourable for pre-emptive action when you are in the first or third seat. When you pre-empt in the first seat it is *possible* that partner has a great hand and you will make life difficult for him. It is more likely that the opponents, with 26 cards to your partner's 13, will hold the balance of power and be the ones to suffer.

The same is true in the third seat. The first two players have denied the values to open and you have a weak hand yourself. The odds are high that the fourth player has a good hand. Now is the time to stretch a bit, perhaps to make a pre-empt on a 6-card suit or on a hand with less than the usual measure of playing strength. For example:

(a) ♠84   (b) ♠92   (c) ♠7
    ♡KQJ1076   ♡Q4   ♡653
    ◇J862   ◇1072   ◇102
    ♣5   ♣AKQ1086 ♣K1087642

If you are third to speak and non-vulnerable, open 3♡ on (a). Should the worst happen and you go four down doubled, the opponents are likely to have a slam on. Most of the time you will not be doubled and it may be difficult for the opponents to find their best contract in the space available.

Pre-empts in the third seat are not necessarily weak. Look at (b). Normally you would open such a hand 1♣, but in the third seat, expecting your left-hand opponent to hold the majors strongly, you should open 3♣. Non-vulnerable in the third seat you might open 3♣ on (c), too. Let the opponents guess which type you have!

Pre-empting at the four level

When you open at the four level you consume so much bidding space that your opponents, with fair values, will often take the money from a double rather than venture into the unknown. You would open four of a major on this type of hand:

(a) ♠AKQJ972 (b) ♠63
    ♡76   ♡AKJ87652
    ◇Q104   ◇9
    ♣5   ♣Q5

At any score open 4♠ on (a) and 4♡ on (b). Note how both hands satisfy the normal requirements for pre-emptive action – good playing strength and little defence. It would be quite wrong to make a pre-emptive opening on either of these hands:

(a) ♠Q1087652 (b) ♠92
    ♡4   ♡AJ87653
    ◇AKJ   ◇A103
    ♣J4   ♣Q

Both hands have good defence and insecure playing strength. Open 1♠ on (a) and 1♡ on (b).

(b) The Opening Lead against a Suit Contract

You may have heard people say, 'When in doubt, lead a trump.' There are situations that call for a trump lead, but in general this maxim is poor advice. Better is, 'When in doubt, lead an unbid suit.'

Hands like the following are dealt by the million:

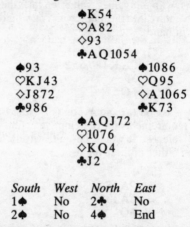

♠K54
♡A82
◇93
♣AQ1054

♠93   ♠1086
♡KJ43   ♡Q95
◇J872   ◇A1065
♣986   ♣K73

♠AQJ72
♡1076
◇KQ4
♣J2

South	West	North	East
1♠	No	2♣	No
2♠	No	4♠	End

West knows that the dummy is likely to contain a fair club suit. He must aim to establish tricks in the red suits before declarer can get dummy's clubs going. His heart holding offers better trick potential than the diamonds, so he leads his fourth best heart – ♡3. Declarer is a doomed man. When East gains the lead with ♣K the defenders will claim two hearts and a diamond.

See what would have happened if West had muttered to himself, 'When in doubt lead a trump.' Declarer would soon have eleven tricks in his pocket. The same is true if West had opened with a club, with the vague notion that 'leading through strength' was a good idea.

Which card to lead

Once you have decided which suit to lead, the general rules for the choice of card are similar to those against notrumps. You lead fourth best from a broken suit, the top of a sequence or an interior sequence, low from three to an honour and the top of a worthless suit.

There are just two differences to remember when leading against a suit contract. First, it is rarely a good idea to underlead an ace. Against notrump contracts it is sound practice to lead fourth best from a suit such as A 10 x x x. You hope to establish the long cards and the ace will act as entry later. Against a suit contract such a lead is hazardous. Declarer may win with a singleton king and you may never score your ace. (Even if the king is not singleton you may be giving up a trick and a tempo.) The second difference is the lead from holdings such as K Q x x x, Q J x x x and J 10 x x x. Against notrumps you would normally lead the fourth best. Against a suit contract you must make sure that your honours play a part in the first two tricks (someone will probably ruff the third round). So, lead the top honour from these combinations.

When to lead trumps

There are some situations when it may be right to lead a trump. One is when you have the great majority of the points and the opponents have sacrificed. Another is when the bidding suggests that you may be able to cut down declarer's ruffs in the short trump hand. Say that the bidding goes like this:

West	East
1♠	1NT
2♡	No

It is quite likely that East will hold one spade and three hearts. You may be able to deprive declarer of a ruff by leading a trump. The same idea applies on this auction:

West	East
1♡	1♠
2♢	3♡
4♡	End

Dummy is likely to hold only three trumps and a trump lead may work well.

When to try for a ruff

A low singleton in a side suit is normally a promising lead, giving good hopes of a ruff. Similarly you may lead from a doubleton honour, such as K x or A x, hoping to find partner with a suitable holding (A x x or K x x). These leads are more dangerous, though, apt to cost a trick when they misfire.

Occasionally, after opponents have bid and supported a side suit, you may be able to judge that partner is short. Then you may lead the ace from such as A 10 x x, or any card from four small when you hold the ace of trumps as a quick entry.

Day Sixteen
(a) The Jump Shift

When your partner opens one of a suit and you jump in a new suit (a sequence such as $1\diamond - 2\heartsuit$ or $1\spadesuit - 3\diamond$), you show a powerful hand and force to game at least. Usually your hand will fall into one of these categories:

(a) it will contain a good suit of its own;

(b) it will have excellent trump support for the opener; or

(c) it will be a balanced hand of at least 16 points.

Strong responding hands with two suits are not handled in this way. You respond at the minimum level, leaving maximum room to find the best fit.

Suppose that your partner has opened $1\heartsuit$ and you hold one of these worthy types:

(a) ♠AQJ976 (b) ♠103
    ♡5   ♡AQ62
    ♢AQ4   ♢A5
    ♣A103   ♣AQJ104

(c) ♠AKJ2   (d) ♠A
    ♡A4   ♡84
    ♢K1032   ♢AK974
    ♣QJ4   ♣AQ852

The first hand, a powerful single-suiter, is a straightforward example of a jump shift to 2♠. Hand (b) contains excellent support for hearts and is too strong for a delayed game raise (2♣ followed by 4♡). Begin with 3♣ and support hearts enthusiastically thereafter.

The first move on hand (c) is a jump to 2♠. Your intention is to bid 3NT on the next round, having already hinted to partner that any slam move by him would be welcome. The fourth hand is certainly very strong, but when you have two suits you cannot afford to consume space by an initial leap to 3♢. Respond 2♢ and continue with 3♣ on the next round. A new suit at the three level is forcing to game.

Opener's rebid following a jump shift

The principles governing the opener's rebid facing a jump shift are similar to those when partner has made a simple change of suit, although the bidding will be one level higher, of course. Imagine that you have opened 1♢ on any one of these hands and your partner has jumped to 2♡.

(a) ♠AQ85   (b) ♠K105
    ♡92   ♡K4
    ◇AK1074   ◇AQJ5
    ♣85   ♣K1082

(c) ♠AK4   (d) ♠Q6
    ♡6   ♡A5
    ◇AKJ1064   ◇AQ1064
    ♣Q72   ♣Q853

No problem on (a). If partner had responded 1♡ you would have
rebid 1♠. Over a 2♡ response you bid 2♠. On (b) you rebid 2NT for the
moment. You will aim for a slam when partner declares his type.

On (c) you would have jumped to 3◇ facing a 1♡ response. There is
no need to jump now, though. Keep the bidding low by rebidding 3◇.
Let partner express his own hand, then you can advance towards
whichever slam looks most promising. On (d) 3♡ is at any rate better
than the alternatives. It is dangerous to introduce a poor suit, like the
clubs here, when a slam is being contemplated.

Completing the auction

One of the main purposes of a jump shift is to investigate the possibility
of a slam without going past game.

West	East	West	East
♠54	♠AKJ973	1♡	2♠
♡KQ1054	♡62	3◇	3♠
◇AQ73	◇KJ4	4♠	No
♣Q3	♣A8		

East has a fine hand, but he has already indicated this. When partner
shows a limited hand (by raising to 4♠) East has no reason to press on.
On the next hand the opener does have values to spare:

West	East	West	East
♠AJ7	♠74	1♡	3◇
♡KQ10862	♡AJ54	3♡	4♡
◇85	◇AKJ95	4NT	5♡
♣A9	♣K2	6♡	No

West has a good trump suit and two aces, so he advances to the slam.
His 4NT call, the Blackwood convention, will be discussed on Day
Eighteen.

(b) When to Cover

When an honour is led to a trick, the next player may need to consider whether he should 'cover' – in other words play a higher honour. The guidance offered in the cradle is 'always cover an honour with an honour'. We will see later that there are many exceptions to this rule. Let's look first at what can be gained by covering. Here is a typical layout:

$$♡AJ108$$
$$♡K63 \qquad\qquad ♡9742$$
$$♡Q5$$

South advances ♡Q. If West covers with the king he will hold South to three tricks in the suit. East's 9 will win the fourth round. By covering, West **promotes** his partner's 9. Had West played low on the queen, South would have continued with a heart to the jack, eventually netting four tricks in the suit. Here is another example:

$$♣AJ83$$
$$♣K74 \qquad\qquad ♣Q92$$
$$♣1065$$

If South leads ♣10, West must cover. Dummy's ace will take the trick and now East will score both the queen and the 9.

So far, covering seems like a good idea. Let's see a few situations when covering can cost a trick.

$$◇QJ8$$
$$◇1063 \qquad\qquad ◇K752$$
$$◇A94$$

Declarer leads ◇Q from dummy. If East covers, South will win with the ace and finesse against West's 10, scoring three tricks. If East lets ◇Q win the first round declarer will be held to two tricks, since East will certainly cover the jack on the next round.

Two general rules for covering have become apparent:

(a) **Cover when this may promote lower cards in your hand or partner's.**

(b) **Do not cover touching cards until the last one is led.**

This second rule has an exception – when your own honour is doubleton you should generally cover the first of touching honours:

$$♠QJ82$$
$$♠1095 \qquad\qquad ♠K3$$
$$♠A763$$

When ♠Q is led you cover with the king. If you play small instead, declarer might continue with a low card from dummy, scoring four tricks.

'How do I know if declarer has touching honours when he makes a lead from the closed hand?' you may ask. Fair enough. Here is a third rule to guide you in that case:

(c) Cover an honour led from the closed hand when there are two honours in the hand to your left; but not when you can see that there is no possibility of establishing a trick in your partner's hand.

Look back at the club and heart positions, where it was right to cover. In both cases the hand to your left held at least two honours.

There are also many situations where a fourth rule comes into play – 'Use your common sense.'

> *North*
> ◇A 7 4
>
> *West*
> ◇K 8 5
>
> *South*
> ◇Q led

Do you cover South's queen of diamonds? No, because there is only one honour to your left (rule c). If South continues with the jack on the next round you will cover then. (If South has led the queen from Q x or Q x x he is either an idiot or a genius.)

> *North*
> ♠J 10 5
>
> *East*
> ♠Q 9 4

Declarer leads ♠J from dummy. Do you cover? No, because you should not cover the first of touching honours (rule b). If declarer held ♠A x x you would give him a second trick by covering.

On the next holding assume that South has opened 1♡ and has been raised to 4♡ by North.

> *North*
> ♡Q 8 5 4 2
>
> *East*
> ♡K 6

Do you cover ♡Q? Remember that the main purpose of covering is to promote lower cards. This is impossible if South has any five-card suit. He may well hold A J 10 x x or (worse) J 10 x x x; you should therefore let the queen pass.

Day Seventeen
(a)   Bidding Slams

To make a slam contract worthwhile, the two hands must contain:
  (a) the playing strength to make twelve tricks, and
  (b) the controls (aces, kings, singletons or voids) to stop the
defenders making two tricks.
  Look at these two hands, for example:

West	East
♠AKJ1082	♠Q94
♡74	♡J5
◇K8	◇AQJ1043
♣AK5	♣Q4

They contain immense playing strength, no fewer than fifteen tricks,
but the defenders can take two winners in hearts.
  Here is the opposite situation:

West	East
♠A1053	♠KQ4
♡A94	♡K82
◇K103	◇A875
♣AK3	♣1086

The two hands contain every control under the sun, but relatively
little playing strength. You would need a fair amount of luck to arrive at
eleven tricks, let alone twelve.
  In most slam auctions the early bids determine that there is adequate
playing strength to make twelve tricks. Subsequently the players
exchange information about the controls they hold. We shall approach
the subject of slam bidding in the same order. We shall see first how to
judge whether you have sufficient playing strength; then, on Day
Eighteen, we shall look at cue bids and Blackwood, the two main
methods for checking on controls.

Bidding slams in notrumps
When you and your partner each hold a flat hand with no long suit you
will need about 33 or 34 points between you to make 6NT a good bet,
around 37 points for 7NT. These are typical auctions:

West	East	Game All
♠AQ92	♠KJ5	
♡K85	♡A104	West East
◇K104	◇AQ3	1NT[1] 6NT
♣KJ3	♣A976	[1]15–17 points

East adds his points to those indicated by his partner. The total is between 33 and 35, just right for a small slam in notrumps. As you can see, the slam is an excellent one. There are eleven tricks on top and the club suit offers good chances for a twelfth.

West	East	Love All	
♠A Q 2	♠K J 3		
♡J 8 2	♡A K 8	West	East
◇A 10 8 4	◇Q J 9	1NT[1]	4NT
♣K 9 4	♣A Q 7 2	6NT	End

[1]12–14 points

Here East has 20 points, so the partnership has between 32 and 34 points. East makes a limit bid of 4NT, suggesting that a slam may be possible. West has 14 points, a maximum, so he advances to 6NT. Take away West's ♠Q and he would let the bidding die in 4NT.

Bidding slams in a suit

When you have a good trump fit for your partner you will find that slams can often be made on many less points. This is particularly true when you have a good second suit that will provide tricks.

West	East	West	East
♠A Q 9 7 2	♠K J 5 4 3	1♠	4♠
♡4	♡K J 7 6	6♠	End
◇A K J 8 5	◇10 3		
♣A 3	♣K 7		

West has two good suits and a powerful hand. When his partner shows a good fit by jumping to game, West jumps straight to the slam. Here it is responder who shows a good suit:

West	East	West	East
♠A K Q 5 4	♠J 10 3 2	1♠	2♣
♡2	♡K 9 4	2◇	4♠
◇A J 4 3	◇9	6♠	End
♣K 4 2	♣A Q J 9 6		

After partner's delayed game raise (an encouraging sequence), West can visualize five tricks in each black suit, plus the ace of diamonds, and surely one more in the wash!

(b) Defending in the Second Seat

In general, 'second hand plays low' is sound advice. Let's see why, with a few examples.

$$♡AQ72$$
$$♡K3 \qquad\qquad ♡10865$$
$$♡J94$$

South leads ♡4. If West plays the king, ('It was dead anyway, partner'), declarer can make four tricks from the suit. He wins with the ace and finesses the 9 on the second round. If West, guided by the general rule, plays low, declarer can make only three tricks.

The same is true here:

$$◇K952$$
$$◇J4 \qquad\qquad ◇Q87$$
$$◇A1063$$

South leads ◇3. If West goes in with the jack ('I wanted to force out the king to promote your holding, partner'), declarer will score four tricks from the suit. He will win with the king and finesse against East's queen on the second round. Playing the jack is pointless.

Even when you can win the trick by playing high in the second seat, it will often cost you a trick to do so.

$$♣K54$$
$$♣A93 \qquad\qquad ♣J107$$
$$♣Q862$$

South leads ♣2. The ace from West would be a calamity!

Often it is right to play low even when you hold two honours:

$$◇AJ92$$
$$◇KQ7 \qquad\qquad ◇1085$$
$$◇643$$

South leads ◇3. If you play the 7 declarer will probably finesse dummy's 9 (which would be the winning play if you held K10x or Q10x). If you are unwise enough to play the king or queen on the first round declarer may escape for one loser. He can win with the ace and return to the South hand to lead towards the jack.

This holding is similar:

$$♡762$$
$$♡J8 \qquad\qquad ♡AK4$$
$$♡Q10953$$

Declarer leads ♡2 from dummy. If you play the 4 he will probably finesse the 10, losing to your partner's jack.

When to play high in the second seat

When declarer has a long suit headed by the ace in an otherwise entryless dummy, you can often make life difficult for him by playing second hand *high*. Here South is in 3NT.

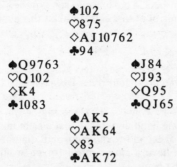

```
                    ♠102
                    ♡875
                    ◇AJ10762
                    ♣94
    ♠Q9763                      ♠J84
    ♡Q102                       ♡J93
    ◇K4                         ◇Q95
    ♣1083                       ♣QJ65
                    ♠AK5
                    ♡AK64
                    ◇83
                    ♣AK72
```

West leads ♣6, drawing the 10, jack and king. At trick 2 declarer plays a diamond to the jack. You can see what will happen if East wins with ◇Q and clears the spade suit. Declarer will pick up ◇K and collect five diamond tricks, bringing his total to eleven. East does better to duck the first round of diamonds, but declarer will still make the contract. With two diamond tricks assured, he will duck a round of hearts. The suit breaks 3–3, giving him nine tricks.

There is only one way to beat the contract. When declarer plays a diamond at trick 2 West must play the *king*. Declarer is now helpless, whether he takes the ace immediately or not.

Day Eighteen
(a) Cue Bids and Blackwood

When you and your partner have agreed a trump suit and it seems that a slam might be in prospect, a bid in a new suit is a **cue bid**, promising first or second round control of that suit. Look at this auction:

West	East	West	East
♠AQ1092	♠KJ54	1♠	3♠
♡A2	♡KJ105	4◇	4♠
◇AQ5	◇K87	End	
♣QJ4	♣84		

West's cue bid of 4◇ conveys these messages:

(a) He has a strong hand and thinks that a slam may be possible.

(b) He has first- or second-round control of diamonds.

(c) He does not have a club control (or he would have bid 4♣, showing his cheapest control).

East can see there are two quick losers in clubs. He signs off in four spades.

You can see how useful it is to be able to suggest a slam without going past game. Here is the same idea again:

West	East	West	East
♠KJ85	♠AQ932	1♣	1♠
♡A5	♡1083	3♠	4◇[1]
◇104	◇KJ	4♡[2]	4NT[3]
♣AKJ105	♣Q84	5♡	6♠

[1] I have a diamond control and it looks as though there may be a slam here.

[2] I can look after the hearts.

[3] Blackwood (see below).

When to bid Blackwood

A call of 4NT (except when it is a direct raise of a natural notrump bid) is **Blackwood**, asking partner how many aces he holds. These are the conventional responses:

5♣ – 0 or 4 aces
5◇ – 1 ace
5♡ – 2 aces
5♠ – 3 aces

A subsequent 5NT call asks for kings on a similar scale.

Many players misuse Blackwood and we will start by looking at two auctions where Blackwood should not have been used.

West	East	West	East
♠A K 3	♠Q 1083	1♡	3♡
♡A K J 1062	♡Q942	4NT	5♢
♢K 4	♢A J	6♡	
♣103	♣J 52		

The slam died an early death when the defenders cashed two club tricks. West's lack of any club control made Blackwood a poor idea. A cue bid of 3♠ would have led to a better auction.

Blackwood is usually wrong when you hold a void:

West	East	West	East
♠K Q J 10742	♠A 93	1♠	3♣
♡K 85	♡A 6	3♠	4♠
♢—	♢107	4NT	5♡
♣A 53	♣K Q J 1072	6♠	End

West could not be sure which two aces his partner held. Fearing that one might be in diamonds, he signed off in six and missed a cold grand slam. It would have been better over 4♠ to bid 5♣, showing a control. When East then bids 5♡ (denying a diamond control), the grand looks a good bet.

Here, at last, is a hand which does lend itself to Blackwood.

West	East	West	East
♠A K Q 1083	♠974	1♠	2♡
♡K Q 4	♡A 10953	3♠	4♠
♢2	♢A J 4	4NT	5♡
♣K 92	♣J 5	6♠	End

West can count plenty of tricks in the major suits. A slam should be easy provided there are not two aces missing.

Many players lose more points by bidding bad slams than they gain by bidding good ones. Slam bidding is a difficult art, which often defeats the professionals. Far and away the best policy is to bid the easy ones and to let the difficult (or unlucky) ones run away.

(b)   Defending in the Third Seat

Those who like to reduce bridge to a collection of maxims stress the importance of playing 'third hand high'. In other words you should usually contribute your highest card when you are third to play to a trick. Let's see the reasoning that lies behind this:

$$♡853$$
$$♡K976 \qquad ♡Q102$$
$$♡AJ4$$

Your partner leads ♡6. You must play the queen or earn a black look from your partner. Similarly:

$$♣95$$
$$♣K10762 \qquad ♣AJ4$$
$$♣Q83$$

Partner leads ♣6. Don't play the jack, a horror known as 'finessing against partner'.

The right play may be different when dummy contains a high card; especially when it is clear that if you part with your own top card you will raise dummy's card to winning status.

$$♢Q72$$
$$♢K9853 \qquad ♢AJ4$$
$$♢106$$

West leads ♢5 and declarer plays low in dummy. If you rise with the ace, dummy's queen will score a trick. You should play the jack instead. You are finessing against dummy, not against partner. As it happens, your partner holds the king, so declarer will make no trick at all from the suit. The play would still be right even if declarer did hold the king, as in this set-up:

$$♢Q72$$
$$♢109653 \qquad ♢AJ4$$
$$♢K8$$

Playing the ace on the first round would give declarer two tricks. The jack restricts him to one. The same principle applies when you hold A10x or even A9x. You do best to play the middle card, retaining the ace to deal with dummy's honour.

The situation is similar when you sit to declarer's left.

```
                    ♠Q92
        ♠AJ104              ♠875
                    ♠K63
```

When East leads ♠8, South playing small, you should play the 10. You know that South holds the king because your partner led a high card ('top of nothing').

Which card to play from equals

When you are in the third seat and have touching cards, such as K–Q or Q–J–10, you should play the lowest of them. This will often give your partner valuable information. Suppose the suit he leads is distributed like this:

```
                    ♣1064
        ♣K975               ♣QJ2
                    ♣A83
```

West leads ♣5 and your jack forces declarer's ace. West can tell that you have the queen, since if declarer held that card he would presumably have won the trick with it.

It follows that when you do play the queen in the third seat you deny the jack:

```
                    ◇875
        ◇K1063              ◇Q92
                    ◇AJ4
```

West leads ◇3 and your queen forces the ace. West can place ◇J with declarer and will realize the danger of continuing the suit if he regains the lead.

Retain useful cards over dummy's strength

Special considerations apply when dummy holds two honours. Look at this combination:

```
                    ♡Q107
        ♡J862               ♡K54
                    ♡A93
```

West leads ♡2, declarer playing the 7 from dummy. If you squander your king declarer will score three tricks in the suit. It is better to play small. Declarer can then make only two tricks under his own steam. Even if your partner's lead was from A x x x, it will cost nothing to duck the first round.

The same is true when you hold J x x over dummy's A 10 x. To play the jack will be fatal when declarer holds Q x x.

Day Nineteen
(a) Making an Overcall

When the opponents open the bidding and you overcall in another suit you may have various purposes in mind:
- (a) to contest the auction, perhaps pushing the opponents too high or reaching a playable spot yourselves;
- (b) to prepare the way for a sacrifice;
- (c) to remove some of the opponents' bidding space;
- (d) to suggest a good opening lead to your partner.

All of these are worthy objectives, which on a borderline hand might induce you to overcall rather than pass. To set against this is the main risk involved, that you may be doubled, either now or later, and lose a big penalty. Also, if you have no chance of obtaining the contract, it may be silly to provide the opponents with information.

The best safety net when overcalling is a **good suit**. Honour cards are not so important; indeed, many overcalls are made on hands that would not be worth an opening bid. Suppose your right-hand opponent has opened 1♦ and you hold one of these hands:

(a) ♠AQJ102	(b) ♠J9752	(c) ♠KJ974
♡843	♡Q53	♡76
♢102	♢74	♢KJ5
♣J74	♣AK5	♣1082

Hand (a) is worth a non-vulnerable overcall of 1♠. You are consuming the opponents' bidding space, depriving them of a 1♡ response. Also, you have a good suit which you would like partner to lead. Hand (b) contains more points than (a), but the spade suit is too weak for an overcall. You should pass. On (c) you might risk a non-vulnerable overcall over 1♣ or 1♦, hoping to shut out an enemy heart fit. Over a 1♡ opening you would pass.

When to overcall at the two level

Two-level overcalls are much more likely to be doubled for penalties than those at the one level. To protect yourself it is particularly important to have a good suit. As a general rule you should expect to go no more than 500 down if you find partner with a poor hand and no fit. Say that your right-hand opponent has opened 1♠ at game all. Which of these hands do you think is worth an overcall?

(a) ♠A2	(b) ♠973	(c) ♠42
♡QJ	♡104	♡AQ765
♢K1082	♢A3	♢J6
♣K9765	♣KQJ1082	♣AQ102

Hand (a) has 13 points, but the club suit is nowhere near good enough for a two-level overcall. If the next player had some clubs sitting over you the carnage might be terrible. The heart shortage makes the hand unsuitable for a takeout double (see Day Twenty-one) so you will have to pass.

Hand (b) is worth a 2♣ overcall at any score. You have six certain tricks and want partner to lead clubs if the opponents win the auction. Hand (c) looks pretty, but it would be unsound to overcall 2♡ on such an empty suit. Some players would risk the call non-vulnerable. You might escape alive, but then again you might not.

When to make a jump overcall

A jump overcall shows a hand too strong for a simple overcall. It suggests about 12–16 points and a strong suit, usually of at least six cards, this type of hand:

(a)	♠AKJ1064	(b)	♠A5
	♡AQ		♡K6
	♢1062		♢87
	♣94		♣KQJ10972

With (a) you would call 2♠ over any one-level opening. On (b) you would overcall 3♣. (One must add, with some regret, that there is also a school that favours weak jump overcalls – on rubbish.)

When to overcall 1NT

When you bid 1NT over a suit opening on your right you show a strong hand, around 16–18 points with a stop in the opponent's suit. These hands would be suitable for a 1NT overcall of 1♡:

(a)	♠K106	(b)	♠AK9
	♡AQ54		♡AJ5
	♢K3		♢KJ1082
	♣KJ92		♣J3

A 1NT overcall in the fourth seat, in an auction such as 1♠ – No – No – 1NT, does not show such a strong hand. Bidding in the so-called protective position will be covered on Day Twenty-six.

(b) Signalling in Defence

When you are following suit and have a choice of small cards to play, you will often have an opportunity to **signal** to your partner. Suppose you have 852 in the suit led. It can hardly affect your trick-taking potential whichever card you play, so use the opportunity to pass some information to your partner.

There are two basic situations where you may wish to signal:

(a) When partner leads to a trick, you play **high to encourage** the lead and **low to discourage** it.

(b) When declarer is playing on a suit, you play **high to show an even number** of cards in the suit, **low to show an odd number**.

We shall look at an example of each signal.

The encourage/discourage signal

Here East uses the signal to indicate his holding in the suit of West's opening lead.

```
                    ♠1073
                    ♡A92
                    ◇K85
                    ♣AKQ8
        ♠AJ9                    ♠4
        ♡QJ103                  ♡8754
        ◇Q103                   ◇AJ642
        ♣1062                   ♣843
                    ♠KQ8652
                    ♡K6
                    ◇97
                    ♣J75
```

South plays in 4♠ and West leads ♡Q, won by dummy's ace. East signals with the 4, his lowest card, indicating his disinterest in the suit. Declarer now plays a trump to the king and ace. West's next play is critical. If West perseveres with hearts declarer will win, cash ♠Q, and turn to the club suit. Away will go one of his diamond losers on the fourth round of clubs. West should *not* continue hearts. He knows from his partner's signal of the 4 that declarer holds ♡K. West should therefore switch to a diamond at trick 3, putting the game one down.

The length signal

When declarer is playing on a suit there are several situations where it will help your partner to know how many cards you hold. One of the most important is where declarer holds a long suit in an otherwise entryless dummy. This is most often the situation in a notrump contract, but here is an example from suit play:

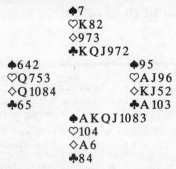

♠7
♥K82
♦973
♣KQJ972

♠642   ♠95
♥Q753   ♥AJ96
♦Q1084   ♦KJ52
♣65   ♣A103

♠AKQJ1083
♥104
♦A6
♣84

South is in 4♠ and West leads ♦4 to his partner's king. Declarer ducks this trick and wins the diamond return. After drawing trumps he plays a club to the king and East must decide whether to release his ace.

If declarer has a singleton club it may be imperative for East to win the trick. If declarer has a doubleton club, as on the present hand, it is essential for East to duck in order to keep declarer to only one club trick. West must therefore signal his club length to assist his partner.

On the present deal West would play ♣6 on the first round, high from an even number of cards. East could then tell that declarer's 4 was not a singleton and would therefore hold off the first round of clubs. South would doubtless ruff a diamond and play a second round of clubs. East would capture and return a fourth round of diamonds, waiting for two heart tricks at the end.

Day Twenty
(a) Responding to Overcalls

When your partner *opens* the bidding with a suit call such as 1♡, you have no clear picture of his hand. His point count might be anywhere from 10 to 20; he might hold four hearts or perhaps seven. It may take several rounds of bidding to determine the best contract. The situation is quite different when partner overcalls. With one call he has provided a fairly accurate description of his hand; at least, you are entitled to make this assumption.

Unless you have a very good suit of your own, your first thought will be how high to go in partner's suit. Suppose that the bidding has started like this:

South	West	North	East
		1♢	1♡
No	?		

On these hands how would you respond to partner's overcall?

(a) ♠A 1054	(b) ♠94	(c) ♠KJ73
♡J62	♡AQ87	♡A 103
♢K983	♢43	♢J2
♣105	♣Q 10752	♣A943

If partner had *opened* 1♡, you would respond 1♠ on (a). That would be quite wrong facing an overcall. Partner has indicated a good heart suit and you should raise to 2♡. On (b) you have an excellent fit with partner. This implies that the opponents will have a good fit somewhere, probably in spades. You should therefore jump the bidding to 3♡, trying to shut out North, who is marked with a good hand. A direct raise to the three or four level tends to be partly pre-emptive.

If your raise is based on high cards and you do not fear competition your first response should be a **cue bid in the opponent's suit**. On (c) bid 2♢. Partner will assume initially that you have a high-card raise to at least 2♡. If he rebids just 2♡, showing a minimum, you will advance to 3♡ on your present hand.

Responding in a new suit

When you bid a new suit, facing an overcall, you show good values. You should not make such a bid to 'rescue' your partner. Suppose the bidding has started:

South	West	North	East
		1♢	1♠
No	?		

What would you call on these hands:

(a) ♠8
    ♡102
    ♢J942
    ♣AQ10542

(b) ♠94
    ♡A1062
    ♢83
    ♣AK1054

(c) ♠Q2
    ♡AKJ982
    ♢Q4
    ♣A104

Don't bid 2♣ on (a) because 'it must be a better contract'. Partner will expect considerably more for such a call, so you should pass. Hand (b) is worth a 2♣ call, but only just. Remember that partner does not guarantee the earth when he overcalls at the one level.

A change of suit is forward-going, but not forcing. Should you be blessed with a hand such as (c), you must jump to 3♡, forcing.

Responding in notrumps

Beware of overbidding when you hold a fair balanced hand facing an overcall. Remember that your partner may not have more than 8 points or so when he overcalls at the one level. Say that East-West are non-vulnerable and the bidding has started like this:

South	West	North	East
		1♢	1♠
No	?		

How much do you think that these hands are worth?

(a) ♠92
    ♡K94
    ♢AJ72
    ♣J853

(b) ♠103
    ♡K76
    ♢AJ53
    ♣Q982

(c) ♠Q2
    ♡A972
    ♢KQ6
    ♣K543

Don't bid 1NT on (a). There is very little chance of a game facing a one-level overcall and you should pass. Hand (b) is minimum for 1NT response, showing about 10–12 points. On (c) you should respond 2NT, no more.

Point-count should not be your only guide in these situations. Obviously you must take note of the score. A vulnerable overcall will be as good as an opening bid, at any rate in playing values. If you are considering notrumps, then a double stop in the enemy suit makes a world of difference.

(b) Keeping in Touch

When you are defending against a notrump contract you will often need to take special steps to maintain communications with your partner. This type of deal is very frequent:

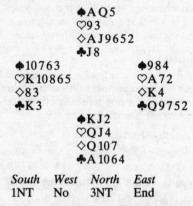

```
              ♠AQ5
              ♡93
              ◇AJ9652
              ♣J8
♠10763                      ♠984
♡K10865                     ♡A72
◇83                         ◇K4
♣K3                         ♣Q9752
              ♠KJ2
              ♡QJ4
              ◇Q107
              ♣A1064
```

South	West	North	East
1NT	No	3NT	End

West leads ♡6 to his partner's ace. Back comes a heart, declarer playing the queen. West has to decide whether he should win the trick or not. You can see that on this deal West will do best to hold off the king. Declarer will have to play on diamonds and East will return another heart when he gains the lead with ◇K.

What if declarer had started with only Q x in hearts, though? It might then prove very expensive for West to hold off the king on the second round. West needs to know how many hearts declarer holds before he can tell whether to hold off the king. It is East's responsibility to furnish this information by giving a count of his own holding in the suit. If East started with three cards he returns the **higher** of the remaining cards. If he started with more than three cards he returns his **original fourth best**.

So on the deal above East returns ♡7 at trick 2. From West's point of view this must be from A72 or A7 alone. There is little prospect of defeating the game if East has the doubleton holding, so West holds up his king and beats the game, as we have seen.

The other side of the coin is shown by this deal:

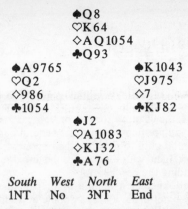

```
                    ♠Q8
                    ♡K64
                    ◇AQ1054
                    ♣Q93
    ♠A9765                      ♠K1043
    ♡Q2                         ♡J975
    ◇986                        ◇7
    ♣1054                       ♣KJ82
                    ♠J2
                    ♡A1083
                    ◇KJ32
                    ♣A76
```

South	West	North	East
1NT	No	3NT	End

West leads ♠6 to his partner's king and back comes ♠3, East's original fourth best. Since this is the lowest spot-card out, West can tell that East did not start with three spades. There is consequently no point in West holding off the ace at trick 2. He takes his ace and returns the suit, the defenders cashing five spade tricks to put the game one down.

A slightly different type of hold-up can be used when partner leads a suit which you hold strongly. Again your aim is to retain your high card as an entry.

```
                    ♠J105
                    ♡J96
                    ◇AQ1087
                    ♣62
    ♠9732                      ♠KQ64
    ♡83                        ♡AK752
    ◇962                       ◇3
    ♣A1085                     ♣743
                    ♠A8
                    ♡Q104
                    ◇KJ54
                    ♣KQJ9
```

South	West	North	East
	No	No	1♡
1NT	No	3NT	End

West leads ♡8 and declarer plays the jack from dummy. To defeat the contract East must allow the jack to win. Declarer has only seven top tricks so at some time he will have to play on clubs. When the moment comes, West will pounce with the ace and return a heart. East's four heart tricks will then put the contract one down.

Day Twenty-one
(a) Take-out Doubles

When your opponents open the bidding in a suit there are three main ways in which you can enter the auction. You can overcall in another suit, you can make a call in notrumps, or you can make a **take-out double**. No doubt you are familiar with the general purpose of such a double. It is not an attempt to penalize the opponent; it tells partner that you have a good hand with support for the unbid suits. It asks him to co-operate in finding the best contract.

How can you tell whether a double is for penalties or take-out? Provided partner has not made a bid, a double of a suit call up to the level of 3♡ is normally for take-out. So, all these doubles qualify:

	South	West	North	East
(a)	1♡	Dble		
(b)	1♠	No	No	Dble
(c)	1♣	No	1♡	Dble
(d)	1♡	No	3♡	Dble

This rule applies even if you have already passed:

	South	West	North	East
(e)	1◇	No	2◇	No
	No	Dble		

	South	West	North	East
(f)	1♡	No	1♠	No
	2♠	No	No	Dble

Both these doubles are for take-out, showing support for the unbid suits and determination to compete when you know the opponents are limited. What sort of hand does a take-out double show? It will often be 4–4–4–1 or 5–4–3–1 with a singleton in the suit that has been opened against you. With this type of hand you can double on about 12 points or more. Each of these hands is a sound double of 1♡:

(a) ♠AJ54	(b) ♠KQ5	(c) ♠KQ104
♡6	♡A	♡A2
◇K1053	◇K9532	◇AQ1054
♣A962	♣Q642	♣83

On hand (c) you have little support for clubs, but if partner responds in that suit you can remove to 2◇, showing this type of hand.

Doubling on a strong hand

When you have an exceptionally strong hand it is usually right to enter the auction with a double, even if your shape is not ideal.

Here are some examples:

West	South	West	North	East
♠AKQ105	1◇	?		
♡Q4				
◇A3				
♣K1054				

You are much too strong to call 1♠, too powerful even for 2♠. Start with a double and bid spades on the next round.

The same principle applies here:

West	South	West	North	East
♠J5	1♠	?		
♡AJ4				
◇AKQ1054				
♣A2				

Again you start with a double. You are far too strong for an overcall of 3◇.

Doubling when the opponents have bid two suits

Suppose that the bidding starts in this fashion:

South	West	North	East
		1♡	No
2♣	?		

A double by West will now show a fair number of points and values in diamonds and spades, the unbid suits. These hands would qualify:

(a) ♠AKJ4	(b) ♠AQ963	(c) ♠AQJ964
♡654	♡7	♡K2
◇AQ102	◇A10754	◇AK5
♣J3	♣92	♣K4

Hand (c) is too strong for a call of 2♠ or 3♠. Start with a double, planning to bid 3♠ on the next round.

So much for making take-out doubles. What about the responses? We will look at that topic on Day Twenty-two.

(b)   Holding up Aces in Defence

An ace is a precious asset when you are defending. Many tricks are lost by defenders playing their aces prematurely. One of the most common situations is when a side-suit singleton is led from the dummy:

5

Q 1083   A 974

K J 62

If East rushes in with his ace he saves declarer a guess. In fact, since most defenders are prone to go in with the ace in this position, declarer will probably guess wrong if you play low without obvious consideration.

Even if declarer holds the king and queen it is often right for East to hold off his ace. This deal is typical:

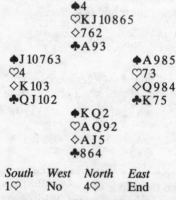

♠4
♡K J 10865
♢762
♣A 93

♠J 10763   ♠A 985
♡4   ♡73
♢K 103   ♢Q 984
♣Q J 102   ♣K 75

♠K Q 2
♡A Q 92
♢A J 5
♣864

South	West	North	East
1♡	No	4♡	End

Declarer wins the club lead and draws two rounds of trumps, ending in the dummy. He then leads dummy's singleton spade. You can see what will happen if East takes the ace. Declarer will subsequently discard two diamonds from dummy on his ♠K Q. Ten tricks will result. If East is smart enough to play low on the first round of spades declarer will lose no trick in spades. He will lose two tricks in each minor, though, going one down.

This is another situation where going in with an ace can cost a trick:

3

K 962   A 1074

Q J 85

The 3 is led from dummy. If East goes in with the ace his partner's king will be exposed to a subsequent **ruffing finesse**. (South will be able to lead the queen, trumping West's king if it is played.)

It is often right to hold up an ace when you sit over dummy's K Q x:

```
            KQ5
   J82             A763
            1094
```

Declarer leads the 4 to dummy's king. If you take the ace, declarer will subsequently finesse the 10, collecting two tricks in the suit. Duck the first round smoothly and declarer will have a difficult guess on the next round.

It can be harder to duck when declarer leads towards honours in the closed hand. Nevertheless, it is often right to do so. In a slam contract, particularly, declarer will rarely lead towards an unsupported king early in the play. Look at this deal, viewed from the West seat.

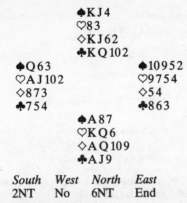

```
            ♠KJ4
            ♡83
            ◇KJ62
            ♣KQ102
   ♠Q63                 ♠10952
   ♡AJ102               ♡9754
   ◇873                 ◇54
   ♣754                 ♣863
            ♠A87
            ♡KQ6
            ◇AQ109
            ♣AJ9
```

South	West	North	East
2NT	No	6NT	End

Declarer wins your diamond lead in dummy and at some point plays a heart to the king. What will happen if you win the trick? Declarer will certainly take the spade finesse, destined to succeed. Duck the first round of hearts and life will not be so easy for him. He will have to guess whether to play on hearts again or bank on the spade finesse.

On this particular deal West can tell, from the bidding, that South must hold the queen of hearts behind the king. Even without direct evidence from the bidding it is usually sound to place declarer with the king-queen in this sort of situation.

Day Twenty-two
(a) Responding to a Take-out Double

When partner makes a take-out double you will normally respond in your longest suit, or in notrumps if you are strong in the suit doubled. That is not the end of the story, though; you must also give him some idea of your strength.

This is a rough guide to the type of response you should make after a take-out double of an opening suit bid.

0–8 points: bid at the minimum level;
9–10 points: make a jump response;
11+ points: cue bid the opponent's suit or bid a game.

We will look at these three cases in turn.

Responding on a weak hand

Suppose the auction has started like this:

South	West	North	East
		1♡	Dble
No	?		

What would you respond on these West hands:

(a) ♠10954   (b) ♠92   (c) ♠10943
    ♡9763   ♡AQ104   ♡852
    ◇85   ◇Q63   ◇KQ102
    ♣J72   ♣10854   ♣Q7

On (a) you bid 1♠, showing your longest suit. It would be a bad mistake to pass, on the grounds that 'you were not worth a bid'. Partner has asked you to bid and a minimum response in a suit guarantees nothing. In any case 1♡ doubled would easily be made. On (b) you bid 1NT, suggesting as a rule around 5–9 points. On (c) you should respond 1♠, despite the diamonds being more powerful. Normally prefer to respond in a major suit when you have a choice of calls.

Responding on an intermediate hand

With the equivalent of 9 or 10 points you may jump in your best suit. This is non-forcing, but invitational. Suppose your partner has doubled an opening of 1♡ and you hold one of these hands:

(a) ♠AQ94   (b) ♠K6   (c) ♠AQJ982
    ♡972   ♡85   ♡1054
    ◇A83   ◇AQJ54   ◇J5
    ♣1054   ♣9762   ♣83

Bid 2♠ on (a) and 3♢ on (b). Hand (c), with its long and strong spades, is worth a jump to 3♠, still non-forcing.

Responding on a strong hand

When you hold upwards of 11 points, game is in sight. If you are not sure of the final denomination you start with a cue bid in the opponent's suit. Say that the bidding has started like this:

South	West	North	East
		1♢	Dble
No	?		

What do you respond on these West hands?

(a) ♠K1082	(b) ♠964	(c) ♠AKJ852
♡AQJ5	♡AQ54	♡64
♢J2	♢AJ2	♢AJ5
♣942	♣K105	♣J3

On (a) you start with a call of 2♢, the opponent's suit. This is a strong call but not forcing to game; it is forcing to 'suit agreement'. If partner bids 2♡ you will raise him to 3♡, non-forcing. On (b) you again start with 2♢. If partner bids hearts you will raise him to game. Otherwise you will bid 3NT on the next round. Hand (c) is too strong for an immediate leap to 4♠. If partner has the right cards 6♠ might be a good contract. Start with a cue bid of 2♢ and jump in spades on the next round. Had your ♢A been ♢Q, an immediate jump to 4♠ would have been correct.

Responding when the opponents have bid two suits

When there is a bid over your partner's take-out double you do not have to speak on a worthless hand. Say that the bidding has started like this:

South	West	North	East
		1♢	Dble
1♡	?		

West may bid 1♠ on modest values such as ♠K10xx and a queen. If West were to bid 1NT, this would show a good diamond stop, not necessarily a heart stop.

(b) Playing a Forcing Game

When you are defending against a suit contract and you hold four trumps, the best line of defence may be to attack declarer's trump holding. You do this by leading your own longest and strongest suit, soon forcing declarer to ruff. By continually plugging away at this side suit you may weaken his trump holding, promoting your own in the process. An example will make this clear.

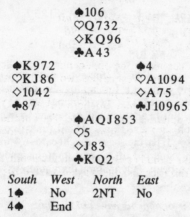

```
                    ♠106
                    ♡Q732
                    ◇KQ96
                    ♣A43
    ♠K972                        ♠4
    ♡KJ86                        ♡A1094
    ◇1042                        ◇A75
    ♣87                          ♣J10965
                    ♠AQJ853
                    ♡5
                    ◇J83
                    ♣KQ2

    South   West    North   East
    1♠      No      2NT     No
    4♠      End
```

West, with four trumps topped by an honour, decides to play a forcing game. He leads ♡6, attacking in his own strongest suit. East's 9 wins the first trick and he continues with ♡4. South ruffs, leaving himself with five trumps. Declarer now crosses to ♣A to take a trump finesse. The ♠10 runs to the king and West returns another heart, reducing declarer to three trumps (the same as West).

Declarer draws the outstanding trumps in three rounds, then knocks out ◇A. East wins and cashes a heart to put the contract one down. The defenders' tactics on this deal are known as **playing a forcing game**.

It is usually wrong to give declarer the chance to ruff in one hand while discarding a loser in the other, but there are times when this type of defence is embarrassing for the man at the wheel.

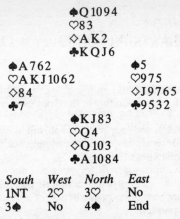

```
                    ♠Q1094
                    ♡83
                    ◇AK2
                    ♣KQJ6
      ♠A762                   ♠5
      ♡AKJ1062                ♡975
      ◇84                     ◇J9765
      ♣7                      ♣9532
                    ♠KJ83
                    ♡Q4
                    ◇Q103
                    ♣A1084
```

South	West	North	East
1NT	2♡	3♡	No
3♠	No	4♠	End

North's 3♡ call, a cue bid in the opponent's suit, indicates a strong hand. South ends in 4♠ and West cashes two heart tricks, his partner suggesting a 3-card holding by playing the 5 followed by the 7. Declarer's 1NT opening marks him with both ♣A and ◇Q, so West can tell that no more side-suit tricks are available. The only hope is to score two trump tricks. At trick 3 he continues with a third round of hearts, giving declarer a ruff-and-discard.

Declarer ruffs with dummy's 9 and continues with the queen of trumps. West ducks this trick and ducks again when ♠10 is played. The trump suit is now like this:

```
              ♠4
      ♠A7            ♠—
              ♠KJ
```

Declarer is helpless. If he plays another round of trumps, West will win and play another heart to remove declarer's last trump. If, instead, declarer turns to the side suits, West will soon score a ruff with ♠7. Note how important it was for West to hold off his ace of trumps until the third round. Had he taken it sooner, declarer would have had a trump left in dummy to deal with a fourth round of hearts.

Day Twenty-three
(a) Third Hand's Action Over a Double

When an opponent makes a take-out double of your partner's opening
suit bid, the principles of responding in third position are different from
normal.

If you have a good fit for your partner you will want to raise him as
high as you can. Your aim is to shut out the opponents, who are likely to
have a similar fit somewhere themselves.

If you do not have a primary fit for your partner you may wish to
advance the auction in some other direction or possibly penalize your
opponents. Or it may be right to pass when after a pass by second hand
you would have responded.

When you have a good trump fit

We shall look first at hands where you have good support for partner's
suit. Suppose the bidding starts like this:

South	West	North	East
			1♡
Dble	?		

What is the best move on these West hands:

(a) ♠954	(b) ♠82	(c) ♠A4
♡Q1082	♡AJ94	♡K1043
♢86	♢962	♢KJ74
♣J932	♣Q1074	♣852

Hand (a) would hardly be worth a call without the opponent's
double. Now you should raise to 2♡, at least occupying one stage in the
bidding ladder and perhaps enabling your partner to compete later. On
(b) you should jump to 3♡. You see the general idea? When you have a
weakish hand with good trump support, bid **one level higher** than you
would have done without the double.

Hand (c) represents a normal sound raise to 3♡. Over a double such
hands are shown by a conventional call of 2NT. This call is not needed in
a natural sense because with a flat 11-count you would start with a
redouble, as we shall see in a moment.

When to redouble

Sometimes, when an opponent doubles, you may think you can
penalize his side. In this case you redouble.

South	West	North	East
			1♠
Dble	?		

You might hold any of these West hands:

(a) ♠84	(b) ♠7	(c) ♠AJ3
♡AQ104	♡AJ	♡AJ972
◇Q972	◇K10532	◇Q1062
♣Q105	♣KQ742	♣5

Hand (a), with just 10 points, is about a minimum for a redouble. Without ♣Q you would call 1NT instead. On (b), too, it is natural for your thoughts to turn towards extracting a penalty. You have only two hearts, but if partner doubles an escape to 2♡ the penalty should be worthwhile. Redouble also on (c). If the next player runs to 2♣ and your partner doubles, you should remove to 2♡ (forcing for one round). Should the opponents alight anywhere else you will double happily.

When to bid a new suit

When you have a fair suit of your own and around 6 points or more, you may bid it over the double. This will give partner a chance to compete in the suit, should the fourth player make a bid. Suppose the auction starts like this:

South	West	North	East
			1◇
Dble	?		

You might hold one of these hands as West:

(a) ♠AQ1085	(b) ♠63	(c) ♠Q9874
♡74	♡AKJ74	♡10752
◇1072	◇K107	◇2
♣942	♣J52	♣K86

Hand (a) does not amount to much, but bid 1♠ nevertheless. This is forcing, as it would be without the double, but no rebid by the opener will embarrass you. If North makes a call as such as 2♡ your partner, with such as ♠Jxx, may be able to compete in spades.

Don't waste time by redoubling on (b). Bid 1♡, commencing a search for your own best spot. On (c) you should pass. It is quite possible that the opponents will stub their toes in a spade or heart contract. (Don't give any thought to rescuing partner from the possibility of playing in 1◇ doubled.)

(b) Trump Promotion

There are various ways in which the defenders can conjure extra trump tricks for themselves. This deal illustrates the most common method:

```
                    ♠93
                    ♡Q1064
                    ◇J75
                    ♣KJ42
        ♠J84                      ♠72
        ♡K5                       ♡AJ82
        ◇10832                    ◇AK64
        ♣9865                     ♣Q103
                    ♠AKQ1065
                    ♡973
                    ◇Q9
                    ♣A7
```

South	West	North	East
			1♡
2♠	No	No	No

West leads ♡K and continues with a second heart to his partner's jack. East cashes a third round of hearts and the two top diamonds, giving the defence the first five tricks. He then plays a fourth round of hearts. Whether declarer ruffs high or with the 10 he will at some point lose a trump trick. West's ♠J has been **promoted**.

Note that East did well to cash ◇AK before playing a fourth round of hearts. Had he omitted this step, declarer would simply have thrown a diamond on the fourth round of hearts.

Refusing to overruff

Sometimes the defenders must refrain from overruffing in order to enjoy an extra trump trick. On the deal at the top of the next page East opens 3♡ and South plays in 4♠. See what happens to West's trump holding.

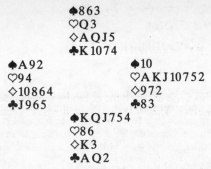

```
          ♠863
          ♡Q3
          ◇AQJ5
          ♣K1074
♠A92                    ♠10
♡94                     ♡AKJ10752
◇10864                  ◇972
♣J965                   ♣83
          ♠KQJ754
          ♡86
          ◇K3
          ♣AQ2
```

West leads ♡9 to East's 10 and East cashes a second round of the suit. Prospects of a minor-suit trick for the defence are bleak from East's point of view, so he continues with a third round of hearts. Declarer ruffs with the king and the spotlight turns to West. If he overruffs with the ace, that will be the defenders' last trick. If West refuses to overruff he will make the ace and eventually the 9, too.

The trump uppercut

When you are ruffing from a short trump holding and you suspect that declarer will overruff, it usually makes sense to ruff with your highest trump. You will force an even higher trump from declarer and possibly promote a trump trick for your partner. That is what happened here:

```
          ♠QJ63
          ♡9854
          ◇QJ5
          ♣A5
♠K10852                 ♠A7
♡J3                     ♡K6
◇A103                   ◇98762
♣986                    ♣J742
          ♠94
          ♡AQ1072
          ◇K4
          ♣KQ103
```

South is in 4♡ and the defenders make the first three tricks with ♠A, ♠K, ◇A. West now leads a third round of spades and East ruffs with the *king*, promoting a trump trick for West.

Day Twenty-four
(a) The Redouble

Say that you bid to 4♡ and one of the opponents doubles you. If you or your partner still feel confident of making the contract you may **redouble**. In practice this type of redouble is quite rare. To make a doubled contract will usually be more rewarding than perhaps driving an opponent back to his own suit. This was West's mistake on the following deal:

East-West game, dealer West

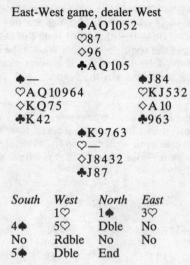

♠AQ1052
♡87
♢96
♣AQ105

♠—
♡AQ10964
♢KQ75
♣K42

♠J84
♡KJ532
♢A10
♣963

♠K9763
♡—
♢J8432
♣J87

South	West	North	East
	1♡	1♠	3♡
4♣	5♡	Dble	No
No	Rdble	No	No
5♠	Dble	End	

West thought, quite rightly, that he had an excellent chance of making 5♡ doubled. He therefore redoubled. Unfortunately for him, South now took fright into 5♠. It turned out that 5♠ could not be beaten. Even if it had gone one or two down, West would still have collected far less than he would in 5♡ doubled. (True, North's double of 5♡ was not from the winning stable.)

The redouble when 1NT is doubled

An opponent who doubles 1NT is very much exposed. If you can count your side for 22 points or more you have them on ice.

Love all

West	South	West	North	East
♠K 10 3				1NT
♡A J 4	Dble	?		
♢8 5 2				
♣Q J 8 4				

You redouble, giving partner the happy news that the balance of the points is yours. You can double anything they say, including 2♢.

The SOS redouble

As we mentioned a moment ago, you will usually have done well enough if you make a doubled contract. For that reason most players have adopted a conventional meaning of redouble *when a part-score in a suit has been doubled for penalties*. In this case only, the redouble is a cry for help. It is known as an SOS redouble and asks partner to try another suit. Here is an example of its use:

West	South	West	North	East
♠2			1♡	1♠
♡A 5	Dble	?		
♢J 10 8 4 3				
♣Q 9 7 6 2				

West makes an SOS redouble. Here it means, 'I don't fancy your chances in 1♠ doubled. Please bid one of the minors.'

This is another frequent use of the bid:

West	South	West	North	East
♠J 9 7 4				1NT
♡10 8 5 2	Dble	2♣	Dble	No
♢J 10 6 3	No	Rdble		
♣2				

West decides that his side will fare better in a suit contract than in 1NT. He pretends at first that he has a club suit. When this is doubled he makes an SOS redouble. Partner will remove to his best suit outside clubs. At least, one hopes so; don't risk it with a beginner.

(b)   Cutting the Defenders' Communications

It is common practice in notrump contracts for declarer to break the defenders' communications by holding up an ace. The same type of play can be made in trump contracts, too:

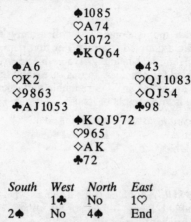

```
                    ♠1085
                    ♡A74
                    ◇1072
                    ♣KQ64
      ♠A6                          ♠43
      ♡K2                          ♡QJ1083
      ◇9863                        ◇QJ54
      ♣AJ1053                      ♣98
                    ♠KQJ972
                    ♡965
                    ◇AK
                    ♣72
```

South	West	North	East
	1♣	No	1♡
2♠	No	4♠	End

West leads ♡K against 4♠. If declarer takes the first trick and plays on trumps, West will win and cross to partner's hand in hearts. Two hearts and the two black aces will put the contract one down.

Declarer should duck the opening lead and win the heart continuation. Now, when the ace of trumps is knocked out, West has no heart to play. Declarer can eventually establish a discard for his heart loser by leading twice towards dummy's ♣KQ.

Even when you have only one loser in the suit led it may pay you to duck the first round to prevent the dangerous hand gaining the lead.

In the deal at the top of the next page South plays in 4♡ after West has opened 1◇.

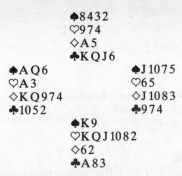

```
          ♠8432
          ♡974
          ◇A5
          ♣KQJ6
♠AQ6                    ♠J1075
♡A3                     ♡65
◇KQ974                  ◇J1083
♣1052                   ♣974
          ♠K9
          ♡KQJ10 8 2
          ◇62
          ♣A83
```

West leads ◇K. If declarer plays dummy's ace at trick 1, West will be able to cross to East's ◇J when he wins the ace of trumps. A spade switch will then defeat the contract. As you see, declarer does better to duck at trick 1.

When a short-suit lead is made against a notrump contract various interesting situations may arise. Look at this deal.

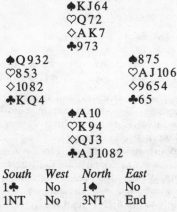

```
          ♠KJ64
          ♡Q72
          ◇AK7
          ♣973
♠Q932                   ♠875
♡853                    ♡AJ106
◇1082                   ◇9654
♣KQ4                    ♣65
          ♠A10
          ♡K94
          ◇QJ3
          ♣AJ1082
```

South	West	North	East
1♣	No	1♠	No
1NT	No	3NT	End

With spades bid against him, West tried his luck with ♡8. Declarer played low from dummy and East's 10 forced the king. Declarer crossed to ◇A to take a club finesse. This lost to the queen and West continued hearts, the defenders taking three tricks in the suit. Declarer's best chance now was a second club finesse, destined to fail.

Declarer could have escaped this fate by playing ♡Q from dummy on the first trick. When East wins and returns the jack, South holds off. Then the defenders take just four tricks.

Day Twenty-five
(a) Two-suited Overcalls

Since a jump overcall (such as 3♣ over 1♡) shows a single-suiter of intermediate strength, we are left with two bids to describe two-suiters: 2NT and a cue bid in the opponent's suit. Both of these can be put to good use.

The unusual notrump

An immediate jump overcall of 2NT shows the two lowest unbid suits and is known as the **Unusual Notrump** convention. You should hold at least five cards in each suit and your hand should be strong enough to give you a fair chance of buying the contract. Suppose the bidding has started like this:

South	West	North	East
1♠	?		

You might hold one of these hands:

(a) ♠6	(b) ♠94	(c) ♠J
♡8	♡2	♡4
◇KQJ82	◇AQ864	◇AKJ1062
♣KJ9653	♣K9752	♣KQ1054

Hand (a) is worth a 2NT overcall, but it would be a borderline decision when vulnerable. You should certainly not bid 2NT on (b), even when non-vulnerable. The hand has little playing strength and two high cards that may work well in defence. Bidding 2NT on this type of hand can work out poorly in several ways. First, you may suffer a large penalty. Second, you warn the opponents that the suits are breaking badly, enabling them to stop low. Finally, you greatly assist them to gauge the play if they eventually win the auction.

Hand (c) is certainly worth a 2NT overcall. In fact it contains rather more playing strength than partner will expect. You can indicate this by bidding over partner's response. If he bids 3♣ you will advance to 3◇, showing a good hand with longer diamonds than clubs. If instead he responds 3◇, you will raise to 4◇.

The Michaels Cue Bid

When the opponents open one of a minor a cue bid in their suit indicates a major two-suiter.

South	West	North	East
1♣	2♣		

or

South	West	North	East
1◇	2◇		

In both cases West shows at least 5–4 (or 4–5) in the majors. The minimum range is a 'good' 8–11 points non-vulnerable or 11–14 vulnerable. When you hold the majors you have more chance to outbid the opponents. Consequently, you do not need such good suits as you do with the unusual notrump. Suppose the bidding starts like this:

South	West	North	East
1◇	?		

You hold one of these major two-suiters:

(a) ♠K 10853	(b) ♠AQ852	(c) ♠AKJ1054
♡QJ972	♡KJ1064	♡KJ854
◇9	◇J5	◇4
♣Q4	♣8	♣9

Non-vulnerable, you might bid 2◇ on (a). Vulnerable you would have to pass. Hand (b) is worth a 2◇ call at any score. On (c) you have values to spare and there may be a game your way. Give partner the good news by raising his response one level.

A cue bid in a major shows a two-suiter consisting of the other major and a minor. The distribution will be at least 5–5. The playing strength should be fairly good, too, since the bidding will often be carried to the three level. Suppose the auction starts like this:

South	West	North	East
1♡	?		

You hold one of these hands:

(a) ♠AQ962	(b) ♠J9653	(c) ♠Q10972
♡J4	♡AK	♡8
◇AJ1054	◇4	◇A
♣6	♣J10742	♣KQJ972

Hand (a) is right for a Michaels 2♡ at any score. Hand (b), with most of the strength outside the long suits, should be passed. Michaels works well on hands like (c), where you have a six-card minor.

When the responder to a 2♡ or 2♠ cue bid wants to know which minor his partner holds, he bids 2NT, always an inquiry in this sequence.

(b) Elimination Play

Probably the most common and profitable form of endplay is elimination play. You eliminate one or more suits from your own hand and the dummy, then give up the lead. A defender will now have to play on one of the remaining suits to your advantage or concede a ruff-and-discard. We start with a straightforward example of the technique.

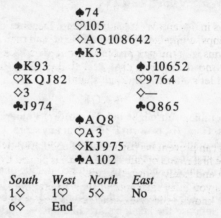

```
                    ♠74
                    ♡105
                    ◇AQ108642
                    ♣K3
        ♠K93                      ♠J10652
        ♡KQJ82                    ♡9764
        ◇3                        ◇—
        ♣J974                     ♣Q865
                    ♠AQ8
                    ♡A3
                    ◇KJ975
                    ♣A102
```

South	West	North	East
1◇	1♡	5◇	No
6◇	End		

West leads ♡K, won by the ace. Declarer draws the outstanding trump, cashes the two top clubs and ruffs a club, thereby **eliminating** the club suit. He then exits with a heart, which West has to win. West has no safe return. A club or a heart will concede a ruff-and-discard (declarer will throw a spade from dummy and ruff in the South hand). A spade return will fare no better, running into declarer's A Q.

Note that for the ruff-and-discard element to be present there must be at least one trump in each hand when the defender is thrown on lead. Here is another example:

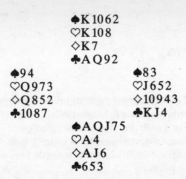

<pre>
                    ♠K1062
                    ♡K108
                    ◇K7
                    ♣AQ92
        ♠94   ♠83
        ♡Q973   ♡J652
        ◇Q852   ◇10943
        ♣1087   ♣KJ4
                    ♠AQJ75
                    ♡A4
                    ◇AJ6
                    ♣653
</pre>

South plays in 6♠ and West leads a trump. Declarer draws a second round of trumps, eliminates both the red suits, and then plays a club to the 9. East wins with the jack and has to concede a trick on his return.

There was no defence on that deal (unless West had led a club initially), but let's alter the club suit slightly:

<pre>
                    ♣AQ82
        ♣1097   ♣KJ4
                    ♣653
</pre>

Now West can prevent his partner being endplayed by rising with the 10 or 9 on the first round of clubs. The queen is played from dummy but East can win and safely return the suit.

Sometimes you must take special steps to prepare a throw-in. One such move is known as **loser-on-loser play**. Look at this deal:

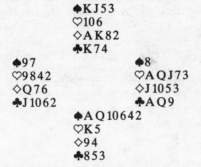

<pre>
                    ♠KJ53
                    ♡106
                    ◇AK82
                    ♣K74
        ♠97   ♠8
        ♡9842   ♡AQJ73
        ◇Q76   ◇J1053
        ♣J1062   ♣AQ9
                    ♠AQ10642
                    ♡K5
                    ◇94
                    ♣853
</pre>

South plays in 4♠ after East has opened 1♡. He wins the second heart, draws trumps, and plays three rounds of diamonds, ruffing the third round. He now crosses to dummy and plays a fourth round of diamonds, throwing a club. East is not a happy man!

Day Twenty-six
(a) Protection

When you are in the pass-out seat you should always think twice before letting the opponents play in a low-level suit contract. Your own hand may not be so great, but if the opponents have stopped low, and you have moderate values, it is reasonable to assume that your partner has values, too. The simplest situation is when an opening one-bid is passed round to the fourth player:

South	West	North	East
		1♡	No
No	?		

You might hold one of these hands:

(a) ♠AQ92	(b) ♠A10972	(c) ♠KQ10872
♡64	♡103	♡4
♢984	♢8543	♢Q105
♣A1083	♣K5	♣A104

On (a) you should double for take-out. In the second seat you would not be worth such a call; in the pass-out seat you can shade bids by about 3 points. Partner will allow for this in his response.

Only 7 points on (b), but that is no reason to sell out to 1♡. North was worth only a one-bid and South could not raise a response. It follows that your partner must hold some values. Bid 1♠. He will not expect very much for a one-level call in the pass-out seat. Hand (c) is stronger and worth a 2♠ call.

The protective 1NT

A direct 1NT overcall normally shows about 16–18 points. In the pass-out seat the requirements are less, more like 10–14 points. The auction might start this way:

South	West	North	East
		1♣	No
No	?		

Each of these West hands qualifies for a 1NT bid:

(a) ♠Q102	(b) ♠K4	(c) ♠J73
♡J54	♡J7	♡A54
♢K1092	♢A9542	♢854
♣AJ5	♣KJ82	♣AQ92

Hand (a) is an obvious 1NT in the protective position. On (b) 1NT is a better prospect than gambling on the straggly diamond suit. Hand (c)

102

contains no direct spade stop but J x x will combine well with various holdings that your partner might have in the suit. Bid 1NT, even when vulnerable. Remember that your partner is marked with a few points. It may have been dangerous for him to overcall directly.

Protecting when the opponents have found a fit

As I have mentioned before, when one side has a good fit so does the other. When the opponents find a fit, yet stop at the two level, you may make two assumptions:

    (a) you have a good fit somewhere yourselves;

    (b) the points are fairly evenly divided between the two sides.

These are two excellent reasons for competing. Indeed you should always be reluctant to let the opponents play in a fit at the two level. This deal is typical:

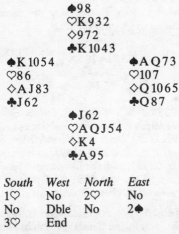

		♠98		
		♡K932		
		♢972		
		♣K1043		
♠K1054				♠AQ73
♡86				♡107
♢AJ83				♢Q1065
♣J62				♣Q87
		♠J62		
		♡AQJ54		
		♢K4		
		♣A95		

South	West	North	East
1♡	No	2♡	No
No	Dble	No	2♠
3♡	End		

West has a moderate collection, only 9 points, but he knows that the odds in favour of competing are good. When East responds 2♠ North-South have two losing options available to them. They can stand by and allow 2♠ to make, or they can advance to 3♡, going one down themselves. These part-score swings are *very* important. They make the difference between being a winning and a losing player.

(b) Reversing the Dummy

In an earlier chapter we looked at the merits of taking ruffs in the short-trump hand. Say you have five trumps in one hand and three in the other: A Q 10 6 2 opposite K J 9. If you can take one ruff with the 3-card holding you will score six trump tricks. To take a ruff with the 5-card holding would generally be unproductive; you would score only the five trump tricks you started with. What if you can take *three* ruffs in the 5-card holding, though? Then you would gain a trick. Three trump tricks in the hand that is short in trumps, plus three ruffs in the other, would bring your total of trump tricks to six.

Such a technique is known as **reversing the dummy**. Here is an example that uses the above trump holding:

```
                    ♠K J 9
                    ♡A 1054
                    ◇K Q 2
                    ♣J 74
    ♠75                            ♠843
    ♡J872                          ♡K Q 93
    ◇J 1064                        ◇95
    ♣K Q 2                         ♣A 985
                    ♠A Q 1062
                    ♡6
                    ◇A 873
                    ♣1063
```

South plays in 4♠ and the defenders start by cashing three club tricks. East switches to ♡K, won in the dummy. It might seem at first glance that declarer needs a 3–3 diamond break to make the contract. He could improve his chances slightly by drawing only two rounds of trumps, then playing three rounds of diamonds. He would then be able to ruff his fourth diamond if the defender with four diamonds also held the last trump.

However, a better line is available – a dummy reversal. Declarer wins the heart switch and ruffs a heart. He then cashes the ace and king of trumps, confirming that the trumps are 3–2. He ruffs a second heart and returns to ◇K to ruff a third heart. Finally he crosses to ◇Q, draws the last trump with dummy's jack and makes the last trick with ◇A.

Count the tricks that declarer made: three diamonds, one heart, three ruffs in the South hand, and three trump tricks in the dummy. A total of ten. Any other line would have failed.

Here is a second example. It is slightly different from the first because declarer's aim is merely to score the small trumps in the long trump hand.

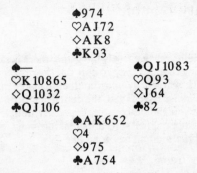

♠974
♡AJ72
◇AK8
♣K93

♠—
♡K10865
◇Q1032
♣QJ106

♠QJ1083
♡Q93
◇J64
♣82

♠AK652
♡4
◇975
♣A754

South plays in 4♠ and wins the ♣Q lead with the ace. He cashes the ace of trumps and is momentarily taken aback when West discards a heart.

From declarer's point of view there now appear to be three trump losers, one diamond loser and at least one club loser. Look at it another way, though. There are five side-suit winners; if declarer can score five trump tricks, this will bring his total to ten.

At trick 3 declarer crosses to ♡A and ruffs a heart. Returning to ♣K, he ruffs another heart. After a diamond to the ace the position is:

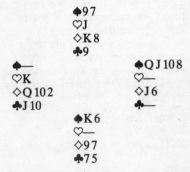

♠97
♡J
◇K8
♣9

♠—
♡K
◇Q102
♣J10

♠QJ108
♡—
◇J6
♣—

♠K6
♡—
◇97
♣75

Declarer leads ♡J from dummy and East is helpless. If he discards, declarer will ruff in the South hand and make two more tricks. If instead East ruffs, South will discard a diamond and subsequently ruff a diamond in the South hand, again bringing his total to ten.

Day Twenty-seven
(a) Penalty Doubles

When the opponents reach a freely bid game, there is rarely much to be
gained by doubling them. If they go only one down your double will not
bring in much. If, warned by your double, declarer makes a contract
which would otherwise have failed, the double has been very expensive.

The only time you should consider a penalty double of a freely bid
game is when the opponents' suits are breaking badly. Suppose you are
sitting West and the bidding has gone like this:

South	West	North	East
1♡	No	2♡	No
4♡	?		

Would you double on either of these hands?

(a) ♠64	(b) ♠7532
♡AK2	♡QJ105
◇J1074	◇9
♣AK53	♣KQJ2

Hand (a) contains nothing unexpected for your opponents, and it
would be foolish to double in the hope of picking up an extra 50 or so.
(South knows he hasn't got the ace-king of hearts or the ace-king of
clubs!) Hand (b), although much weaker than (a), represents a sounder
penalty double. The opponents were not expecting to lose two trump
tricks and the singleton diamond may cause an upset as well. Also you
have a good lead – the club king, *not* the diamond singleton.

The situation is similar when you are considering a double of 3NT.
Suppose the bidding has gone:

South	West	North	East
1♠	No	2◇	No
2♠	No	2NT	No
3NT	?		

How would you rate a double on either of these West hands?

(a) ♠A94	(b) ♠KJ1072
♡AQ8	♡A64
◇Q96	◇5
♣KJ32	♣J1082

To double on (a) ('I had 16 points, partner') would be a beginner's
mistake. Declarer will have no problem in establishing the spades and
the diamonds. It is quite possible that he will score one or more
overtricks. Hand (b), though, represents a promising double. Your

spades sit menacingly over declarer's long suit and it is quite likely that your partner has something good in diamonds. Also, you know that neither opponent has anything in reserve because both North and South made a *limited* bid on the second round. In view of your double partner may well lead a spade in preference to a diamond from some such holding as Q 10 x x x.

Penalty doubles of part scores

The biggest penalties come not from games and slams, but from low-level overcalls. A player who makes a simple overcall at the two level is stepping into the dark, with little idea of what his partner holds. He will often have no more than four or five tricks in his own hand. If he finds a blank hand opposite, you may be able to take a large penalty. That's what happened here:

Game all, dealer East

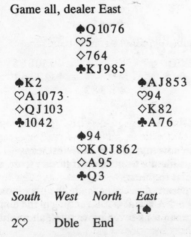

```
              ♠Q 1076
              ♡5
              ◇764
              ♣KJ985
♠K2                      ♠AJ853
♡A 1073                  ♡94
◇QJ103                   ◇K82
♣1042                    ♣A76
              ♠94
              ♡KQJ862
              ◇A95
              ♣Q3
```

South	West	North	East
			1♠
2♡	Dble	End	

West, with two trump tricks and no certainty of scoring game in his own direction, made a penalty double of 2♡. He attacked in diamonds and declarer won the second round. When the queen of trumps was led West won with the ace, cashed the third round of diamonds and switched to king and another spade. East won with the jack and returned a third round of the suit. This ensured two more trump tricks for the defenders and an 800 penalty. It was good business on a combined point-count of 22.

(b) The Cross-ruff

In most trump contracts declarer will draw trumps at some stage during the play. Sometimes, as we have seen, he will delay this step if he first needs to take some ruffs in the short-trump hand. There is one type of hand where declarer does not draw trumps. Instead he aims to score the trumps in each hand separately, by taking ruffs in both hands. Here is a straightforward example of the play, which is known as a **cross-ruff**.

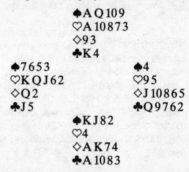

```
              ♠A Q 10 9
              ♡A 10 8 7 3
              ◇9 3
              ♣K 4
♠7 6 5 3                    ♠4
♡K Q J 6 2                  ♡9 5
◇Q 2                        ◇J 10 8 6 5
♣J 5                        ♣Q 9 7 6 2
              ♠K J 8 2
              ♡4
              ◇A K 7 4
              ♣A 10 8 3
```

South reaches an adventurous 7♠ and West leads ♡K. Declarer can count five tricks outside the trump suit. If he can score all eight trumps he will bring his total to thirteen.

When this deal occurred declarer made the play look easy. He won with ♡A and cashed ◇A K and ♣A K, ending in the dummy. He ruffed a heart with the 2, then took seven more ruffs, alternating between the two hands.

You may have missed one essential manœuvre that declarer performed. He cashed all his side-suit winners *before* embarking on the cross-ruff. If, after winning the heart lead, he had continued by cashing the top clubs and ruffing a club, West would have discarded a diamond. Declarer would no longer be able to score both his diamond winners and the contract would fail.

Note also that West could have beaten the slam by leading a trump. Against grand slams a trump lead is usually the best idea.

Try this hand in 6♣:

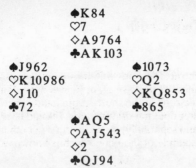

```
                      ♠K84
                      ♡7
                      ◇A9764
                      ♣AK103
    ♠J962                        ♠1073
    ♡K10986                      ♡Q2
    ◇J10                         ◇KQ853
    ♣72                          ♣865
                      ♠AQ5
                      ♡AJ543
                      ◇2
                      ♣QJ94
```

West leads ◇J, won in the dummy. You can rely on eight trump tricks from a cross-ruff, so you need only four side-suit winners. Cash the red aces, followed by just two top spades. You can then ruff diamonds and hearts alternately, eventually scoring twelve tricks.

As you see, you can actually score thirteen tricks on this deal by cashing *three* rounds of spades before starting the cross-ruff. You might play a grand slam in this fashion, but it would be a silly risk to take in a small slam. If the spades were 5–2 one defender might ruff the third round of spades and return a trump, putting your contract at risk.

Day Twenty-eight
(a) Defence to 1NT

When the opponents open a weak notrump there is no reason to sit idly by, leaving the auction to them. You can overcall in a suit or you can double for penalties.

Suppose that your right-hand opponent has opened a 12–14 notrump and you hold one of these hands.

```
(a) ♠KJ10962    (b) ♠J9763
    ♡10             ♡A52
    ◇AQ72           ◇A104
    ♣84             ♣K8

(c) ♠A3         (d) ♠A64
    ♡KQJ102         ♡A732
    ◇972            ◇AQ
    ♣AK4            ♣10765
```

No problem on (a); you bid 2♠. Your excellent suit will protect you from a sizeable penalty, even if the player sitting over you has a strong hand. On (b) the spade suit is poor. There is little to be gained from bidding; you might run into a heavy penalty. Suppose you pass and the left-hand opponent bids 2◇ or 2♡, it will then be relatively safe for you to compete with 2♠ when the bidding runs round to you.

Hand (c), and most hands of 15 points or more, should be launched with a double. This is a penalty double, indicating a wish to defend. On (d) you have no good call. It would be unthinkable to bid one of your 4-card suits and you are not quite strong enough for a penalty double, especially as you have no reliable lead.

When partner's 1NT is doubled

When your partner's 1NT opening has been doubled and you hold a weakish hand, you may wish to seek a haven somewhere. Suppose the bidding starts like this:

South	West	North	East
			1NT (12–14)
Dble	?		

You might hold one of these hands:

```
(a) ♠103      (b) ♠74       (c) ♠Q83      (d) ♠A1092
    ♡85           ♡Q8742        ♡10742        ♡72
    ◇Q974         ◇AJ43         ◇965          ◇AK84
    ♣J8652        ♣93           ♣1073         ♣973
```

On (a) you run to 2♣. After a double this call is not Stayman: it is more important to have an escape route into clubs. Hand (b) is not particularly weak, but it is safer to bid 2♡ than to pass. On (c) you expect to go down in 1NT, perhaps heavily. There is nowhere better to go, though, so you pass. With (d) you know that your side has the balance of the points. You redouble to give partner the good news. If the fourth player runs for cover, your side can double him.

When partner has doubled 1NT

This is another critical situation.

South	West	North	East
		1NT	Dble
No	?		

What is the best move on these West hands?

(a) ♠A94	(b) ♠J82	(c) ♠J962
♡852	♡Q9765	♡1064
♢103	♢4	♢982
♣K10852	♣10862	♣873

Absolutely no problem on (a): your partner has indicated at least 15 points and you have two good cards yourself. Pass happily, hoping to land a big penalty. With (b) it is best to take out partner's double to 2♡. This is a weak call. If you had any values, as in (a), you would leave in partner's double. Hand (c) puts you in an anxious position since you fear that 1NT doubled may succeed. Nevertheless, there is nowhere better to go. Partners can sometimes defeat the contract, particularly with the advantage of the opening lead. If they make overtricks, blame partner!

When partner's 1NT has been overcalled

Suppose your partner opens 1NT and the next player makes a bid such as 2♡. You have several options open to you. Double would be for penalties; a new suit at the minimum level (such as 3♣) would be competitive; and a cue bid of 3♡ would be a game force, inviting partner to show a spade suit or bid 3NT.

(b) The Throw-in

When you have an ace–queen combination, finessing the queen will give you a 50–50 chance of success. Obviously it is better if you can arrange for the opponent sitting over the tenace to lead the suit. He will then have to lead *into* the ace–queen, making two tricks certain.

Such a play is known as a **throw-in**. Here is a straightforward example:

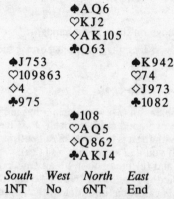

```
              ♠AQ6
              ♡KJ2
              ◇AK105
              ♣Q63
♠J753                      ♠K942
♡109863                    ♡74
◇4                         ◇J973
♣975                       ♣1082
              ♠108
              ♡AQ5
              ◇Q862
              ♣AKJ4
```

South	West	North	East
1NT	No	6NT	End

West leads ♡10, which you win. You test the diamond suit and find that East has a winner there. This leaves you with eleven top tricks and the spade finesse as apparently the best chance of a twelfth.

There is another possibility, though. If you can remove East's clubs and hearts, you will be able to throw him in on the fourth round of diamonds.

You cash four rounds of clubs, followed by the two remaining heart winners. As it happens, East shows out on the third round of hearts. These cards remain:

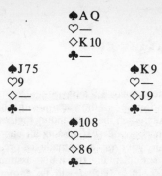

When you cash ♢K and exit with a diamond, East has to give you two spade tricks.

Here is another example. The principle is the same. You remove the defender's safe exit cards, then throw him in, forcing him to concede a trick with his return.

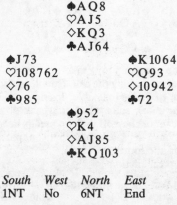

South	West	North	East
1NT	No	6NT	End

You win West's club lead, noting that there are eleven tricks on top. There are finessing possibilities in both the major suits. What if East has both the missing honours, though? A throw-in will be possible if you can remove his holdings in the minor suits. You start with four rounds of diamonds, throwing a club from dummy. After three rounds of clubs you will know that East has only major-suit cards left. Now a spade to the 8 (or cover West's jack with the queen) will assuredly leave East on play, forced to return a heart or a spade.

Day Twenty-nine
(a) Defence to Pre-empts

Your right-hand opponent opens 3♡ and you find yourself looking at a reasonable hand. Should you enter the auction at this high level? If you do, you risk a big penalty when the outstanding high cards are stacked on your left. If you do not, you risk missing an easy game or slam. Awkward, but that is why your opponent made the pre-empt in the first place. In general you should make the initial assumption that your partner has around 8 points. If that will be enough to make life comfortable for you at the level you will have to play, go ahead and enter the auction.

The best defence against pre-empts is also the simplest – the **take-out double**. Suppose it is love all and the player to your right opens 3◇. What would you call on these hands?

(a) ♠AQ104	(b) ♠K104	(c) ♠K7
♡AJ93	♡AQJ54	♡9643
◇62	◇7	◇AQ95
♣K64	♣AQ93	♣A62

Hand (a) is about a minimum for a take-out double. Vulnerable, you might think twice before making the call. Double is also the best call on (b). The alternative of 3♡ is inflexible, losing out when partner has length in one of the black suits. One drawback of playing take-out doubles is that you cannot chop off the opponent's head when you hold a hand like (c). You have to pass, hoping that your partner will have the strength to double in the fourth seat.

Here are some typical auctions:

West	East	South	West	North	East
♠AQ105	♠K9742	3◇	Dble	No	3♠
♡KQJ4	♡103	No	4♠	End	
◇6	◇Q53				
♣AJ102	♣764				

West cannot guarantee ten tricks on his own hand, but there is no reason to place partner with a blank hand. He advances to the spade game, which proves to be an excellent one.

West	East	South	West	North	East
♠AK84	♠Q10972	3♡	Dble	No	4♠
♡62	♡85	End			
◇AQ86	◇K96				
♣QJ7	♣A82				

East, with a well-disposed 9 points, takes the responsibility of bidding game himself. Had he called only 3♠, his partner would have had no sound reason to advance.

When to bid 3NT

An overcall of 3NT suggests a balanced hand of around 18–22 points, but the call is sometimes made when holding a long minor suit. These hands are all suitable for a 3NT overcall of 3♠.

(a)	♠A Q 4	(b)	♠Q J 4	(c)	♠A 5
	♡A 2		♡A 9 3		♡J 4
	◇K Q J 4		◇K 2		◇A K Q J 8 2
	♣Q 10 7 3		♣A Q J 10 4		♣K 6 3

How to bid a two-suiter

The best tactics on a two-suiter depend on various factors. Look at these examples:

West	South	West	North	East
♠A K 10 7 5	3◇	?		
♡Q 4				
◇6				
♣A K J 5 4				

Here a double is fairly safe. If partner responds 3♡, you can bid 3♠, indicating the two black suits and fair values.

West	South	West	North	East
♠K 3	3◇	?		
♡A Q J 8 2				
◇10				
♣A J 7 5 4				

A double is not so attractive here because a 3♠ response would be awkward. Best is a simple overcall of 3♡.

When the opponents open at the four level

A double of 4♣ or 4◇ is primarily for take-out; a double of 4♡ or 4♠ suggests a strong hand, not just trump tricks. 4NT is always available if you want partner to bid.

(b) Trump Coups

Suppose you are playing in a trump contract with a trump suit distributed like this:

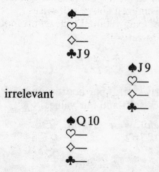

♠A 2

♠6   ♠J 974

♠K Q 10 8 5 3

Unless gifted by second sight, you will doubtless start by cashing the ace and king of the suit. It will no longer be possible to pick up East's jack with a straightforward finesse, but sometimes you can achieve this type of end position:

♠—
♡—
♢—
♣J 9

                       ♠J 9
                       ♡—
irrelevant   ♢—
                       ♣—

♠Q 10
♡—
♢—
♣—

You lead a club from dummy and East is deprived of his trump trick. Such a play is known as a **trump coup**. The end position above might arise from this deal:

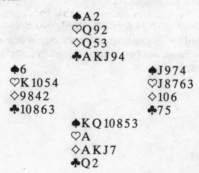

♠A 2
♡Q 9 2
♢Q 5 3
♣A K J 9 4

♠6   ♠J 974
♡K 10 5 4   ♡J 8763
♢9842   ♢106
♣10 8 6 3   ♣75

♠K Q 10 8 5 3
♡A
♢A K J 7
♣Q 2

South arrives in seven spades and West leads ◇2. Declarer notes that all will be well if trumps are 3–2 or the jack falls singleton. If East has four trumps to the jack a trump coup will be needed.

Look back at the end position South must strive for and you will see that he has the same trump length as East. This is a necessary feature of this type of ending (otherwise South would have to ruff at trick 11 and the lead would be in the wrong hand). So, declarer will have to *ruff twice* in the South hand to reduce his trump length to that of East.

How does the play go? South's ◇A wins the first trick and declarer cashes ♡A. He now plays the king and ace of trumps, putting the lead in dummy. When East shows up with J x x x in trumps declarer ruffs a heart, returns to ◇Q and ruffs another heart. He now holds Q 10 in trumps to East's J 9.

Declarer cashes ♣Q and crosses to ♣A. The final step is to run dummy's club winners. If East ruffs at any time, declarer will overruff, draw the last trump and claim the balance. If instead East refuses to ruff, the end position visualized above will arise.

Here is another type of trump coup. Declarer promotes his last trump by leading a plain card towards it.

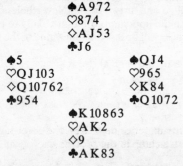

```
              ♠A 9 7 2
              ♡8 7 4
              ◇A J 5 3
              ♣J 6
    ♠5                      ♠Q J 4
    ♡Q J 10 3               ♡9 6 5
    ◇Q 10 7 6 2            ◇K 8 4
    ♣9 5 4                 ♣Q 10 7 2
              ♠K 10 8 6 3
              ♡A K 2
              ◇9
              ♣A K 8 3
```

Playing in 6♠, the declarer soon finds that the trumps are 3–1. He must then aim to ruff two diamonds in hand, two clubs in the dummy. When declarer leads a fourth diamond from the table East will have to ruff (allowing South to dispose of ♡2) or to discard, letting South make a trick with his last trump.

Day Thirty
(a) Sacrificing

Suppose you are sitting West at love all and you hold this hand:

♠ A K 8 5 4 2
♡ 9 4
♢ Q J 8
♣ K 3

What should you say after this start to the auction:

South	West	North	East
	1♠	2♡	2♠
4♡	?		

You have to judge whether you should bid 4♠. First you must ask yourself, is 4♠ likely to make? Not really. It is *possible* that partner has a singleton heart and ♢K, and that ♣A is well placed. It is much more likely that you will go one or two down. Nevertheless, it is right to bid 4♠. Why? Because the opponents are quite likely to make 4♡ and the penalty in 4♠ doubled will be less than the value of the game they would have made.

A call such as 4♠ on the hand above is known as a **sacrifice** bid. Such calls may gain in various ways:

(a) You may actually make the contract;
(b) the penalty you suffer may be less than the value of the opponents' contract;
(c) the opponents may decide to bid one level higher themselves, possibly overstretching in the process.

Making an advance sacrifice

Whenever you and your partner have a good trump fit, so will the opponents. Why is that? Because they will both be fairly short in your own suit, correspondingly long in the other suits. It follows that when your side does have an exceptional fit you should try to shut the opponents out of the auction. Here is a typical example:

West   North–South game
♠ K 9 4
♡ 8 2 | South | West | North | East |
♢ 1 0 6 2 |-------|------|-------|------|
♣ K Q J 8 4 | | | | 3♠ |
                    | No | ? | | |

Bid 4♠. You don't expect to make it; indeed, you will probably go two down. What is almost certain is that the opponents can make at least a game in one of the red suits.

This situation is similar:

West · · · · · · · North–South game
♠K 10854
♡92 · · · · · · · · *South* · *West* · *North* · *East*
◇105 · · · · · · · · · · · · · · · · · 1◇ · · · · 1♠
♣Q1072 · · · · · · 2♡ · · ?

Again you should bid 4♠. This will make life very awkward for the opponents. If they double you the penalty will be poor compensation for their vulnerable game. If they bid on, there is always the possibility that they will go down.

Making high-level decisions

Suppose that you have bid a vulnerable 4♡ and the opponents, non-vulnerable, have sacrificed in 4♠. It may be that they will go only one or two down and that you can make eleven tricks in hearts. In that case you would obviously do best to advance to 5♡.

When the 4♠ call is immediately to your right you have three options. You can *double*, which means you have a clear preference for defending. You can *bid on*, if you have sufficient extra playing strength to expect to make eleven tricks. The third option is to *pass*, leaving the decision to your partner. This is a common situation:

East–West game
South · *West* · *North* · *East*
· · · · · · · 1♡ · · · 1♠ · · · 4♡
4♠ · · · · ?

As West, you might hold any of these hands:

(a) ♠82 · · · · · · (b) ♠3 · · · · · · · (c) ♠9
♡A 10852 · · · · · ♡AQJ94 · · · · · · ♡A 10754
◇KQ4 · · · · · · · ◇K2 · · · · · · · · ◇AQ92
♣KJ7 · · · · · · · ♣A 10965 · · · · · ♣KJ5

On (a) you have no playing strength to spare and would not welcome a five-level contract. You should double, expressing a clear preference for defending. Hand (b) offers every expectation of making eleven tricks in a heart contract. You should therefore call 5♡. (There would be no point in showing your second suit.) Hand (c) fits somewhere between the two other hands. You have a singleton spade and if partner chose to bid 5♡ rather than double you would be happy to play there. You should pass, leaving the decision to your partner.

(b)   The Simple Squeeze

When one defender has the sole guard in two of your suits you can often put him under pressure in the end-game. Look what happens to West here:

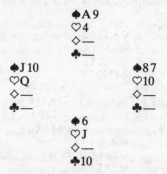

```
            ♠A 9
            ♡4
            ◇—
            ♣—
♠J 10                    ♠87
♡Q                      ♡10
◇—                      ◇—
♣—                      ♣—
            ♠6
            ♡J
            ◇—
            ♣10
```

You lead ♣10 and West must surrender one of his guards, giving you an extra trick. This type of play is known as a **squeeze**. This form of play gives rise to many complications, but in its simpler forms it is quite easy to execute.

The end position above had three important components that are present in almost all squeezes:

   (1) The **squeeze card** (♣10), the card that you play to force a crucial discard from the defender.
   (2) A **threat card (or menace card) accompanied by a winner** (♠A 9). This usually lies in the hand opposite the squeeze card.
   (3) A **single threat card** in another suit (♡J).

The ending might have arisen from this deal:

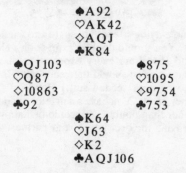

```
            ♠A 9 2
            ♡A K 4 2
            ◇A Q J
            ♣K 8 4
♠Q J 10 3               ♠875
♡Q 8 7                 ♡10 9 5
◇10 8 6 3              ◇9 7 5 4
♣9 2                   ♣7 5 3
            ♠K 6 4
            ♡J 6 3
            ◇K 2
            ♣A Q J 10 6
```

You reach 7NT and win the lead of ♠Q with your king. There are twelve tricks on top and a thirteenth can be made if ♡Q falls doubleton or if West (who surely started with ♠QJ10) also holds ♡Q.

You cash ♡AK but no queen appears. Then you play three rounds of diamonds, throwing a spade from the South hand. Finally you run the club suit. On the last club, as we saw in the end position above, West is squeezed.

Here is another squeeze hand. See if you can identify the squeeze card, the threat card accompanied by a winner (a two-card menace), and the single threat card.

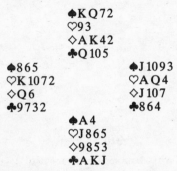

```
              ♠KQ72
              ♡93
              ◇AK42
              ♣Q105
  ♠865                    ♠J1093
  ♡K1072                  ♡AQ4
  ◇Q6                     ◇J107
  ♣9732                   ♣864
              ♠A4
              ♡J865
              ◇9853
              ♣AKJ
```

You reach 3NT and West leads ♡2. The defenders cash four tricks in hearts and West switches to a spade, which you win with the ace. How would you plan the play?

You have eight tricks on top and the only chance for a ninth is to find the same defender guarding the spades and the diamonds. You cash ◇AK, setting up your ◇9 as a single *threat card*. Dummy's ♠KQ7 represents the *threat card accompanied by a winner*. It only remains to cash three rounds of clubs, the last of which will be the *squeeze card*.

If East doesn't understand how you made the contract, you can always recommend that he buys this book!